Brian

The Guide To Vasilias

Copyright © 2024 Jeremy F. Paul All rights reserved

They ate her. Consumed her in front of me. The horde. I watched helplessly as they stripped Iana's flesh from her muscles. Then muscles from bone. They ate until all that was left were the hollow, marrowless bones of the woman I loved. Cherished.

It has been 155 days since then.

She should have been on a ship. Any ship. There was more than enough room. But they shut their fucking doors as we ran to the staging area. I will remember those chubby faces as long as I have eyes. I know I never will, but I hope to one day repay their cruelty. Not everyone that was left behind chose to be soldiers. We had to become soldiers because we were left behind. Ill equipped soldiers.

The horde cannot fly. They do however move extremely fast. They are keeping hostages. Treating them like my mother told us that humans treated animals. Making them mate, to have more to feast on. They feed the captives charred pieces of the dead to fatten them up. I guess the computers see us as lesser beings like we saw every other animal back on Earth. We have become the rats. Roaches. Running away when we hear them coming. You can tell the horde is coming by the whistle of them moving. Iana was a singer. Said that the sound was a C5. Something that you'd hear on the videos about opera singers.

The last few days have been unspeakable. The last 9 years have been horrific. The horde of murderous and parasitic bugs and nanites have grown innumerable all over Mars. In the canyons and underground caves. The grasslands. The other World carriers departed, leaving us with one ship and a rather finite fuel source. The horde had been overtaking the settlements, only sparing the women. It was death to everyone else. The leadership decided to send soldiers, then drones, RCP's. The horde was victorious over everything. So the leaders ordered evacuation. They made sure they were already onboard. Cowards.

The horde seems genuinely angry that the ships got away. They have been killing everyone left behind at their leisure. That, or capturing us. I was captured once. They spent 3 hours trying to eat me. That felt like a million emery boards rubbing against my skin at the same time. And fast. But I have my mothers skin. Lucky me. Then the horde made me watch as they ate the other soldiers that tried to rescue the hostages with me..

I walked naked, back to the tunnels. Where they wouldn't go.

Iana's eyes were the most beautiful things I could have ever been lost in. I adored how wide they would get in the mornings when she would first see me. Light brown. Almost hazel. They were framed by her dark lashes. Long. Natural. Her tribal makeup only accentuated her eye.

Above her otherworldly eyes were two lovely eyebrows. Every detail of her face rests heavy in my memories. Her soft, plump cheeks. They always danced when she laughed. Iana was insecure about her forehead, so she normally covered it with her hair. Her hair, curly. Soft. Reddish brown. Like the sky when a dust storm is approaching. I loved the way it smelled when she got out of the shower. She used to stare out of the window after her showers and her hair would be, at least temporarily, reddish. It would smell like earth grass or sunflowers.

Her nose was my second favorite part of her body to kiss. The curve of her nostrils leading to her smile. I miss her smile lines.

Her mouth was wide and full. A perfect bottom lip. Pouty. Plump. Which she covered with pink gloss often. Her upper lip wasn't large, but also was not thin. Her chin that soft round, small chin. Shaped like the curve between my thumb and index finger. I wanted to spend forever looking at her face. Making her laugh.

Her voice was light, but filled with conviction. Hearing her say my name was the best start to my days. She was the best part of my day. Every day.

My mother, when I was 10, told me that humanity would probably be dead within the next hundred. That the planet had already started to poison its inhabitants in an effort to get rid of its problem. Humans, said she had tasted it in the air for at least a century. That it would be bad. Then she looked over at my sisters, who were too young to understand what she was saying, and pulled a series of large notebooks out of a satchel next to her. She opened up the first one to a random page and had me read it. What I read was her confession of killing a glass maker, In Italy, almost 800 years before. In brutal detail. How she jammed both of her daggers into his shoulders. Watched him struggle to breathe and how she laughed while he drowned in his own blood. Sadistically. How she enjoyed the kill. Then she dragged the man's body to the shore and threw him in.

When I looked up from the page, I saw her face and she said to me "Brian, I am immortal. And you will be too."

She let me read all of her writings. All of her stories. I learned so much about her life and was frightened by her childhood. I asked her some dumb questions and my sisters jumped in with the same. I didn't know what to ask of her. Then she told me that I had a brother. He lived in Africa. A giant, long lived man. She called him and we all talked every day for a week. It took me 3 months to finish reading everything. Learning that the immortality is temporary for all of her children, that didn't feel good. That some didn't live long enough to get it. Some, One lived a full life without ever having it. Just mom got to live forever. To be perfect. Then she began teaching me to fight. Secretly, while father was at work. She showed me all of the different fighting styles that she had several lifetimes to perfect.

Once the government announced the lottery and world carriers, mom just hoped one of us could make it onto them. The lottery took place 8 months after my 18th birthday. Had they held the lottery before I turned 18, my sisters could have come with me. My whole family could have come with me, had I been younger. I remember being mad about it, but mom got me alone and told me that I must go. To live on. On the day she took me to the drop off point, she told me that if I live long enough, maybe we'll see each other again. Then she gave me a notebook. Told me to get one 3-D printed every 6 months. I journal now because of her. Because my immortality kicked in when things started going bad. When the micro computers and artificial intelligence thought the best option was to join the side of the insect-like horde and try to eradicate all living creatures. To start over and populate Mars naturally.

There's only a handful of us left. Myself and six others. The horde has captured or killed everyone else. We turned off the power to the ship and the location magnetics to be invisible to their ways to locate us. There are 3 medics, 2 pilots, 1 actual soldier and myself. They are all I could stop the horde from taking. They once came with a hostage and threatened to kill her in front of all of us unless I traded 10 of the people for her. A young female hostage. There were only 19 of us left. So we tried to fight. We lost. 12 soldiers died as did the little girl, so that we could make it to the ship and get away. The last soldier lost his arm and his rifle. He later found their stronghold, the Hebes Chasma. Its where they are holding everyone. He said there were thousands of people. He watched for 3 days until he couldn't anymore. The horde were doing public executions of anyone that wasn't able bodied. If they had so much as a cold, they were killed. Namely the children. Then they'd force the women to mate with another able bodied man under threat of killing their remaining child or first lover. Whatever word exists that means machine version of chattel slavery, is what is happening according to that soldier. He returned with the horror stories 3 days ago. The 6 remaining all know I am immortal. That the horde can't harm me. They've seen it.

But throwing punches at small organisms and nano-machines, will get me no where. None of us are brilliant strategists. But we 7 are tired of losing and would rather die in battle trying to free the enslaved than die on the run, in fear of them finding who is left.

The next 10 days, one way or the other, will mark the end of humans on this planet. The 7 of us have put together a plan to rescue as many as we can and then leave this cursed planet. The nano-machines have a schedule they keep. We've tracked it. There is a small window to be able to convert this plan. They are prepared to lose their lives to save the others. The pilots have taught me how to start the engine on the ship in case they don't make it out. They all expect me to make it out. They know I will.

We make it out, we head to the new world. The nights are full of death. We hear the screams. We will end this.

Myself and a legless Róisín, we are the last of the 7, the rescue team. We failed to rescue everyone. We only were able to save 309 humans, out of the countless men, women and children we freed. That's how many made it onto the ship before I detonated the payload from the ground. The ship had taken off.

Some of the 309 carried Róisín onto the ship and put her in the pilots chair. The horde was closing in and crippling everyone that was running towards the ship. I threw a little girl on board before the door closed, then I ran towards the screams of the people being consumed by the horde with the payload hidden under my clothes. I looked back and saw that the ship was out of the canyon. Then detonated. Killed everything around me. What was left around me.

I crawled to the rendezvous. When the ship came and picked me up, I was greeted with fear and awe. I'm going to have to make a speech. We were given coordinates, and instructions. They decided on a world. The other ships. Quaternary Star system. So we are headed that way.

Róisín has been using the coordinates that the other ships sent back and the starline from the ancient satellites, to navigate. It has been 9 years. We left Mars 9 years ago. News from Earth is that Mars has been overrun by the remnants of the horde. They have consumed all the structures we humans left behind on the surface. To what ends? I don't know why, but I'm glad to be off the world.

We have 417 people on board now. A lot of children have been born. It took 6 months to get clothing made for everyone. The children have been learning about space and physics. Two of them have ideas of how to improve F.R.A.M.E. I have been sitting in on the classes that the new artificial intelligence teaches the children. All parents are weary of computers, so we have a ship full of involved parents. We, all aboard the ship, won't be betrayed by them again.

Roisin died today. She was my friend. Her daughter has taken over duties. Calls me Uncle Brian. Roisin taught her how to pilot the ship. Her body is going to be placed in the terrarium like all of the dead. We are approximately 31 light years away from the new world. The settlers have sent us the specs on how to improve F.R.A.M.E to its full potential. They also left markers in the form of Sat's at each gravity heavy spot. What should have taken us 300+ Earth or Mars years, will take 82 more years instead. Imair thinks she can shave 20 more years off that. She's 19, and like her mother. I hope she's right. She wants to see the new world.

The passengers on board have begun to realize they probably won't live long enough to see the new world. There have been a rash of suicides. I had to give a speech. Make assurances and promises. They look to me as a leader.

The original rescued have begun to die of old age. Their children are also old.

The generation after that are without hope. 60 more Earth/Mars cycles will be needed before we make it to the world they call, Vasilias.

Imar told me that she cannot trim time safely and without passing through a dark nebulae. She wants to see the new world badly. Judging her for being impatient would be wrong. Judging anyone for their impatience under the circumstances would be disgraceful.
I have time, they do not. She has lived over 271,000 hours. The equivilant of close to 31 years of earth time. She is with child, her dream; Roisin's blood, will continue.

Betelgeuse is barely visible now. The smartest among us says that it should fade from view in time through the Jing Nebula cloud. Espescially where we are going. Imar's twins are eight earth years. Fraternal. Boy and girl. They love the stars. They don't realize the life they have coming. 52 years until we land on Vasilias. The satellites that lead our way have been a great deal of help. Imar and Oshem have worked out that the gravity wells that the first travelers used have gotten more volatile. Stronger. than when they used them. They hypothesize that they can shave 18 years off the travel time. Construction of a transport using F.R.A.M.E. has finished. It is capable of carrying two thousand people. There are less than 1300 on board!

What I feared would happen, did. The horde were hiding on the ship, for 101 years. They laid dormant, undetected and hiding in the aquarium for 101 years. There should have been signs. We never heard them. They made no noise. All of these years of thinking we were safe, that we escaped. I couldn't have been more wrong. Prevailing theory is that they hid in the hair and keepsakes of the original escapees. Then activated when we went through a magnetic gravity storm 600 or 700 hours ago. The ship had lost power completely. Survival mode kicked in for the horde, likely. We were able to reboot after a few minutes, and once we did get the ship online, the massacre had begun.

618 of our number lost initially. They cornered half of the survivors in the cargo hold and Imar was among them. She made the sacrifice and opened the doors. Everybody and the horde were sucked out into space. There are 713 of us left. Most of which are children.

I activated the artificial Intelligence to do a full sweep of the ship. Every corner, pipe, jacket pocket, scalp or grave. Checked and cleared. Inside and outside of the ship. We are off course and need to course correct. The corpses of the 618 first killed will be cleaned and converted to engine fuel, at least until we pass through the Garmee cluster. I have no choice but to let the AI navigate our way to Vasilias. All of our pilots and navigators are dead. It will take a decade for one of the apprentice children to learn how to exploit F.R.A.M.E. and follow the path given to us. I instructed the children that when we make it to the new world, that keeping the secret of my immortality would be important. We should arrive there, if the computers are correct, in 26* years. I will have to make sure they all make it. Are educated and trained to survive. To know history. To appreciate the life, they are going to have.

We have been following the regimen as told by the other ships. Increasing the gravity, gradually over the last 20 years, in an effort to prepare the people on the ship for the gravity on Vasilias. We've been told of the life on the planet, the monstrous flying creatures and the even more frightening sea life. They say that they have tried to establish communication channels with some animals, but they have avoided us humans. I can understand why.

We've also been told the world is huge. Beyond huge. Bigger than even our former light giver. They've had 29 years and have really not explored much of the planet. But each world cartier has decided to claim land on the many different continents. Some things never change.

The star system that houses and sustains Vasilias, our new home is a mass of chaos. 4 stars, 16 planets. A gas cloud is currently covering the lower brown dwarf. Everything seems to be drawn towards the bright giant at the center. On the far end of the system is a fairly sized white dwarf.

Vasilias, passes between the Giant and the dwarf. It is the largest, non-star entity in the system. The worlds in this system are a mix of beauty and horror. The worlds closer to the Giant are essentially fireballs being eaten because they are too close to the giant. Pieces of the three worlds randomly break off and float towards the star, in flames, to be consumed.
The next 5 worlds are small lifeless husks. Deserts. Deserted worlds, too hot

and irradiated to be hospitable on the surface. My science officers theorize that these planets will likely spawn life or possibly hold life in their poles. One of the worlds, the one just before Vasilias, is so eclipsed by the size of the worlds before and after it that it is a dark blue, almost black color. The rotations, annual cycles, of these worlds vary as their paths are not just circular, but ovals. Prevailing sentiment is these worlds, the final seven worlds will all collide with each other at some point. The world we passed first, looks to be an oasis, that weaves its way through all four of the stars. It narrowly misses each of the outer planets that are pulled too close together by the white dwarf.

I hope it survives that crunch of planets.

The stars appear attracted to each other but are repelled by their fields. This is a strange system. I'm not even sure the scientists are right. It should take us 12 and a half years to arrive at our new home. 6 if we get a good slingshot on the dwarf.

The population already on the planet have gone radio silent to us. The people of our transport aren't a military. The last of the military was Roisin. The AI couldn't teach us how to do military things so we focused on philosophy and science. Humanitarianism. I taught all who wanted to learn how to defend themselves hand to hand or staff fighting like mother taught me.

Everyone on the ship is prepared for their new home. Most want to go live in whatever nation is the most peaceful. I assume when we are closer to the planet that someone will begin to tell us where to set our transport down. Then they'll go their separate ways.

My own plan is to explore the planet, like Mom did with Earth. Over 150 years of being on a ship, hurtling across all of the galaxy, I'm just excited to see something, anything more than this. The darkness of space.

We're about to land, the government calls itself A.P.C. Even on a new world they chose borders and division. A.P.C. opened communication as soon as we were in upper Atmosphere. They said that we entered over their airspace, but gave us clearance.
The population of the transport, final numbers: 1316 women. 974 males.
They gave me a tablet to journal with as a going away gift. I'm going to use it to track things and places. They have promised not to expose my secret. I'll enter my written pages into records, my records. At least until I figure out how to make paper and ink while on a land that doesn't or maybe does have all of the resources I'm used to.
Its a long life ahead. Here's to a future without the mistakes of humanities past.

68 Y.A.A.

Continent: Known only as The Animal Kingdom.

Capital: Ruling animals reside in Highland Cave.

Leader: Two Stomps. An animal that can only be described as a 6 legged, 3 tusked, 2 trunked Woolly Mammoth. Cold blooded animals. His kind is said to live many centuries.

Type of Government: Tribal Council/ Dictatorship

Type of Law System: Kratocracy / Merit based law.

Population: The entirety of the Animal Kingdom's population is innumerable. It's human population is less than 3,000 as of 59 Y.A.A.

Elevation: Highest point: 347,932 feet. High Mountain.
              Lowest point: -2145 feet. Caves of Big Lake

Geography: 41.48 million square miles of land.
              Area of Big Lake 766,167 square miles.
              Most common tree: Stomp Wood

The humans that have colonized this planet have somehow forced all of the very large native animals onto this, the world's largest continent which they have called Animal Kingdom. While the continent is bigger than all of Earth's, it seems sort of inhumane to pile creatures from different continents and islands off of their lands and onto one piece of land, but that's humanity. I was told that their method of capturing and transporting was done safely and with cooperation, but knowing the greed that exists of my kind, that is untrue. The process took 11 Earth years. Still fresh. The smaller creatures, they have tried to domesticate to varying levels of success. These small animals seem intelligent but are docile like dogs and cats. Most of the smaller animals on this planet resemble Earth mammals, but are lizards. Everything on this world is still carbon based but it appears that other than the mammals that were brought on the world carriers, there aren't any other mammals.

I've been told that there are more than a few monstrous creatures on this world that appear mammal-like and that I would find them on the animal continent. Our own animals that we kept and bred from Earth and Mars that survived the siege of the horde, if they were apex on our original worlds, they deposited them on Animal Kingdom. If they were trainable, they were kept among the humans and farmed for food while the settlers tried to figure out how to transform this new soil into something that would take our plants.

Most of the animals from our home worlds that survived the trip through space could not take the new gravity and had to be used for food. They were kept on the world carriers in an environment of gravity control. The strong were able to leave the ships.

The first native life form I encountered on this continent were the Prae. Large, flying lizard-like animals with faces resembling earth rodents. Thousands of them. They sit in the overgrown forests that surround the shore, watching everything and attacking anything that gets too high in the air. They make flying drones to look ahead impossible. Due to them, in the 68 years since humans arrived on this world, they've not been able to accurately map the terrain of this particular continent. The views from space are often obscured by the light of the 4 stars and the lack of light on the ground. And the Prae are strong enough in flight to reach the clouds. The creatures native to this land are intelligent. They have their own hierarchy. The Prae aren't very vocal and appear to communicate by body positioning. None of us humans have heard them make any noise. But they are organized and obey the largest of all of them. After the large forests that line common shores, is the marsh lands. This is where various insectoids, small and large, live alongside lizards that resemble dinosaurs from the movies. The settlers introduced tortoises, crocodiles and monitors to this land, and they appear to have been able to find their way. Their niche.

There are hundreds of different dinosaur-like creatures that walk around, that appear both mammalian and reptilian by sight. Beasts that resemble hairy 20 foot high elephants, but have too many legs, tusks and trunks. 70 foot snakes with thagomizer spikes on the ends of their bodies. Centipedes as big as buses. Scale covered, wolf-like creatures as big as automobiles. All of the native life forms on this continent look angry, toothy, frightening. But on this continent, they obey a hierarchy of the strongest animal rules. These creatures, don't just communicate with their own species, they communicate with each other. Vocally. I've heard the mammal-like ones hissing like the reptilian animals and vice versa. Each creature is seemingly capable of speaking another creatures language, verbally. I have not been allowed audience with the elephant/mammoth like creatures as they live in the caves midway up the cliffs. The trail to them is sound, but the creatures guarding their entrance are toothy, poisonous and with incredible distrust of humans. Pressing the issue could mean the death of the 3000 or so humans they allow to live on the continent.

At night, all of the Vasilian creatures come out of hiding and stare at the stars. Each staring at one of the distant stars or moons that they can see. There is an aurora that occurs nightly over the northernmost area of the continent, like a rainbow in the night skipping across the sky. Caused by the tidally locked moon, it dips and covers the mountaintops, giving off a reflection on the ice. I've never seen anything like it. They get to peacefully admire it every night.

The earthquakes on this continent are small and seasonal. The hot springs usually signal when they are coming by the eruption of multiple geysers. The natural wonders on this continent, the pure rivers, bottomless lakes, cliffs and caverns are bigger than anything human eyes have seen. Every mountain here is bigger than Everest. In the middle of the continent is a mountain range with a lake of ice at the top. I tried to make the trip, but the air is thin and I'm not strong enough yet. The ice cascades like a waterfall periodically when it warms up. There is so much of this planet to see just here. I think I might take forever to explore this world.

Hard Tail
Tail
Has spikes

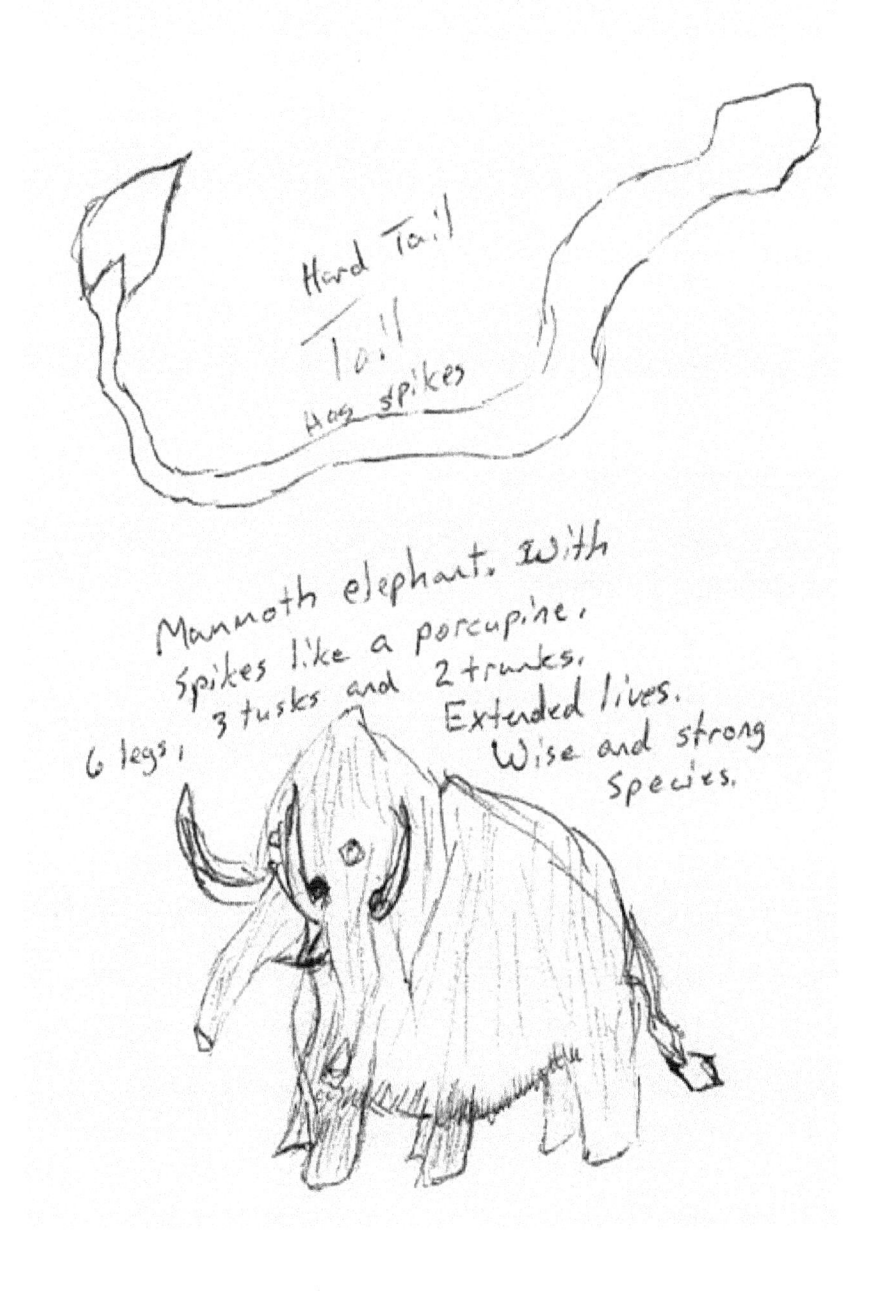

Mammoth elephant. With spikes like a porcupine. 6 legs, 3 tusks and 2 trunks. Extended lives. Wise and strong species.

148 Y.A.A.

Continent: Salta de Argentine

Capital: Santa Messi

Leader: Francis Saurez

Type of Government: Constitutional Dictatorship

Type of Law System: Common

Population: 2.7 Million

Elevation: High Point: Mount Peron 94 kilometers
　　　　　　Low Point: Green Valley -214 feet

Geography: Southern half is uninhabitable on the surface in the cold zone. The government built caves to go underground in the cold zone. Pure water river, immeasurably deep, flows across the center of the continent. The government is building infrastructure across the northern half for open air living and advanced architecture.
　　　　　Most common tree: Erlat Derna

I was contacted by Oriah, the grandchild of Olondra and told of the APC military officials commandeering the ship under a false accusation. I had been assured that our ship was safe to house outside the capital, but I guess I should have stayed vigilant instead of trusting the human government. After experiencing over 90 years of the Animal Kingdom's hospitality and civility, going to a human government full of liars and dishonorable minds has been disappointing. Even if the generation I encountered was honorable, the next might not be. I must remember that in the future.

The governments of this continent and others have fallen into distinct Earth behaviors. It is as if they watched the historical records of the old times and decided that was what they wanted this world to be. Here, they use lies and propaganda to build trust in the military and the overseers. Predictive policing to harass the people they want gone off of the continent. Then fear and hatred to unite their citizens against everyone else. Namely, the Animal Kingdom. Two Stomps, the leader of AK, told me that the reason the Prae live on the outskirts is to prevent the human governments nearby from trying to survey the land. Because each land they surveyed previously, they took from the animals. APC, now known as Salta De Argentine, was no different. I was shown many destroyed and armed drones, thrown into a pile by the great mountain. All of them had Argentina's colors on them. Arrogant bastards.

Oriah told me that most of the people from my ship had found a way off of the continent after the government sent troops, began forcing everyone into citizenship and harassing them into patriotic loyalty. They took away my people's sovereignty to have control of two ships instead of one. One more than the other nations had. Which has made my objective clear. I am going to get back on the ship, offload the data and give command to the AI to fly to the northern moon until I see fit to call it back. After that, I will ask Two Stomps to grant asylum to my people's descendants who want to escape this place. And if any wish to stay here, then I wish them well.

Having the AI travel with me should have been priority number one. But, I didn't think ahead. Maybe it was my experience with the horde. Not wanting technology anywhere near me. But now I understand that I need to make sure this nation doesn't get to use our ship, to make themselves the premier world power or wage war against the Animal Kingdom. That war seems to be an increasing possibility with the rhetoric that I've encountered in my second trip to this land. When we first landed it was different. The people were patriotic, but not bigots. Now, they have become nationalists. 4 generations and they've devolved into being hate filled segregationists, trying to be this worlds extreme super-power. I should have taken heed of my mothers warnings about Spaniards, because that is the main language spoken here. I will not forget her lessons anymore.

I should be able to meet up with Oriah's contact midway up the coast to take the river to camp. I think this will be tough and getting out will be tougher, but long term, this will work out in the best interest of this world. Their military lives in cities built into cliffs on the coasts and hillsides. It is law that everyone between the ages of 10 and 30 has to serve in their military. The lowlands are forests of orange bark. The southern point, cold. Too cold for human life to function normally. So, I need to have my alibi's in order before I attempt this, it'll be hard to avoid military detection. When we first landed, we were informed that each settlement had written their own constitutions. They began to share them digitally whenever you enter the border. The following text is my best attempt to translate Salta's.

SDA Constitution

We, the people of Cortez y Soto decree upon settlement that we are a nation built and founded upon freedom, security and self-preservation. Any and all affronts upon our people, constitutes an act of war should our appointed president and prime minister decree.

Entrance to our lands constitute contractual agreement to abide by our laws. Disobeying our laws, will be grounds for immediate deportation, and if the laws you break are one of the natural laws, it can result in your death.

Natural laws include - No violence unless sanctioned; no theft, mutual respect.

1. Every citizen natural is required to own a weapon and is, at the age of 10 cycles, active military.
2. No person who was not born on this land can ever be a full citizen, with benefits. Only partial citizen.
3. Government, at the Federal level, has the power, right and ability to revoke citizenship, to anyone who proves themselves unworthy.
4. Non-citizens are not guaranteed any of the rights afforded the natural born.
5. In an effort to continue growing the population, life is deemed to begin at first heartbeat. Abortion will be illegal, for all reasons except the health of the woman, in our nation, for a term of 1,000 years post settlement.

177 Y.A.A.

Continent: United Nations of America

Capital: Constitution

Leader: Pr. Juan Williamson. PrM. Estelle Renault

Type of Government: Democratic Republic

Type of Law System: Judicial

Population: 3.83 million

Elevation: Mount Washington 133,717 feet
              Vale de Pele – 3,119 feet below ocean level

Geography: Lake Earth surrounded by Vale de Pele. Southern Quarter is in uninhabitable zone, but is seasonally inhabited and has underground cities. Mountain range is spiraled. Mount Washington is the highest outer peak. No large rivers, small rivers coming from the lake stretch all across the continent.

              Most Common Tree: Tengai Kyodaina

I remember that my mother told me about how the United States of America was, for more than 500 years, the premier world power on Earth. That they destabilized, genocided, assassinated, enslaved and installed puppet governments in other nations for centuries. Took what they wanted. Made their citizens turn on each other and their government. And the weirdest part was that there wasn't a clandestine group in charge. No cabal. No Illuminati. No puppet masters pulling the strings. It was simply the people taking advantage of the people and blaming the people. They created a causality paradox of idiocy and shielded it with victim-hood. When everyone left mars and settled here on the continent of their choosing, there weren't just United States descendants. There were people descended from all of the America's. North and South. Canada to Chile. Many of the people that were left behind on Mars to fight were male Muslims, the Chinese and the United States military. What was left on the America's ship were the learned. Teachers, politicians, environmentalists and entertainers. Almost all devoid of military prowess. When they landed on this world, they came to a realization that they needed a fighting force. Their carrier lives were a model for how they wanted civilization to be, but the other ships were building empires, not utopias. They were well over a century behind.

I am told that when they chose this continent, that they did so by fooling the other ships into believing they still had military might.

That they were warriors instead of pacifists. They used the fear of the past to get all of the other ships to relocate the native animals to establish the Animal Kingdom. Their first political leader was an actor that chose the name Arthur Reebe. I met him towards the end of his life while I was on the AK. He told me that he knew the secret of the animal natives first. That they weren't just scary monsters. That they were verbal. That they could easily understand our languages. And the ones with tongues could speak them if taught. Fluently. Arthur had retired to the Kingdom to teach English, Spanish and Portuguese to Two Stomps and anyone else that would like to learn. In secret. For this favor, the animals of this planet vowed to share knowledge of the world with the U.N.A. Arthur then introduced Two Stomps to several allies he had made in his time as president that he knew weren't warmongers or hateful of the native life. They were sworn to secrecy and shared their languages with the animals who in turn granted them "rugut" or a lifetime of truce.

The continent and the people themselves on it are ordinary. They work out constantly and make updated versions of movies made centuries ago with artificial intelligence. They haven't gotten a real military put together yet. They have begun constructing monuments as they continue to explore the land to give the impression of the old ways. Each nation has claimed areas and have begun constructing large artistic pieces in celebration of their national heroes. Lake Earth is deep, dark and in the center of the continent and is also surrounded by hot springs while situated in the shadow of a monstrous cluster of mountains. The mountains spiral around each other for miles with the center mountain standing straight up and through all of the mountains. The resulting cave system with its various pathways makes it a beautiful sight to observe and explore. The downside for most of the humans is the frigid temperatures at the top of the mountains as well as the inability to fly over it commercially.

Their current leadership is almost a mirror to how life was on Earth. There are elections, terms and governmental stagnation. However, they went with a President and a Prime Minister. The President of the moment is a man named Juan Williamson and the Prime Minister is named Estelle Renault. They seem genuinely into bringing peace and innovation to their various countries. They have made themselves into the melting pot that their namesakes so steadily pursued as a constitutional surface goal. And the people don't hate the people.

281 Y.A.A.

Continent: Ahravshk/Shaanti/Trade Hub

Capital: Representation Hill. (No real Capital)

Leader: Various representatives and trade Ambassadors.

Type of Government: Republic

Type of Law System: Voluntary honor system.

Population: 126 humans during peacetime, can be up to 1800.

Elevation: Ajagar – 21,733 feet
　　　　　Ahravshk point – 141 feet

Geography: Tsunami sized waves attack hills, very hilly. Roller coaster type terrain. Entire coastline is a desert except south eastern point. Rest of the continent is dense forest. Animal Kingdom has caves in all of the hills as their shelter.
　　　　　Most Common Tree: Erlat Derna

The combined numbers of allies to the Animal Kingdom decided to come together on the volatile land mass nearest to AK to form a trade coalition in an effort to show the other human leaders that these weren't animals like our Earth/Martian animals. It took years to convince the leadership of various nations, but we did it. When we finally achieved a consensus, I took the idea to Two-Stomps. He took a few hours to think it over, before calling together the heads of the land he ruled. That was just to explain the word, trade. Animals had no need for trade. It was a kratocracy. Strongest of all, leads. So, the question that myself and my protege, Andits, had to answer was "What do you have, that we'd want, that we could not just take if we wanted it." My answer wasn't satisfactory, not initially. Information, responsibility and kinship among other things. Two Stomps asked me to explain the other things.

I tried to explain that my word was eternal. That being my friend, being loyal to me, means that I would be loyal to him and his kind until he drew his last breath due to his kindness. That I did not take his charity for granted. And even if he wronged me in the future, I would at least allow for a chance at reason afterwards. That all of those people that I brought to the table believed that being a friend, was much more important and beneficial than being their enemy. And if needed, we would fight on their side in any battle that was just and fair. Two Stomps informed us that while being a friend was nice, and that he appreciated the gesture, that the kingdom he ruled was much bigger than we could realize. He would later tell us that the only reason that all of the native life had willingly gotten onto the human ships and come to his land was because he ordered it so to add distance between them and the new diseased animals with the weapons. The alternative to not getting on the World Carriers was waiting on the sea life to bring them to the land, which can take entirely too long. The humans allowed him to unify his vast kingdom at once and in one location while thinking that they were grabbing land. They did not plan ahead. And Two Stomps has led me to believe that there are plenty of terrifying secrets about this world that humans aren't aware of.

I was able to convince Two Stomps eventually, who then convinced his kingdom of the plan to unite with a select group of the humans. The agreement was to meet on the continent nearby. A distance that is a 3 hour journey from the shore for him. Two Stomps doesn't understand the need for any ambassadors, because he refuses to let anyone speak for him. His rule is his rule alone. He demanded all of the ally nations swear to send their leaders to the trade table if he was summoned to show up. No subordinates. Everyone has agreed. And that was the birth of the name The Trade Land.

The entire trade continent is a series of hills. Not many areas of plain land, just large, constant hills and deep sweeping valleys. The hills themselves might all be dormant volcanoes because the tops are usually leveled-off craters. There are caves, likely from whatever meteor showers happened long before, burrowed into the sides of some of the monstrous hills, each of which is decorated with orange colored grasses and weird tree roots that grow out of the sides of the land yet along the ground. All of the nations have agreed that on the highest of the hills with the flattest top, that is where the embassies and consulates will be built and stationed. They have prepared to build 16 buildings, to plan for a future that includes all of the nations and continents on a site they are calling Representation Hill. But for now, it is just 6 of them. Two-Stomps demanded that his accommodations be built into the caves, but would not say why. The nations obliged. The river that runs through the continent carves a strong path and carries the rapid moving waves from the nearby and violent ocean throughout the land. There is no basin, just one continuous surge of water starting from the mouth of the river until it reaches the shore of the other side of the continent. Scientists say that the water should have eroded the hills bare, but the water comes from a fresh water hot spot. The roots of the trees that grow along the hills stick out into the passing water, taking in the nutrients, but resisting the heat. That river is one of many fresh water sources on the planet. From above, the fresh water appears to be a deep blue color as opposed to the salty light blue of the other water sources.

Coming to and from the Trade Land in the future will be a chore due to the constant tsunamis striking the shores between itself and AK when the Panacea moon passes. The mixing of the fresh and salt water with its resultant atmosphere spawns heat storms, tornadoes and volatile hurricanes over the water. Two-Stomps told me that he will travel to any meetings between the nations the way he does normally. His kingdom will provide.

393 Y.A.A.

Continent: Sovereignty

Capital: Camelot

Leader: Elmer Windsor, King of Sovereignty, Descendant of Markle and Harry Sussex.

Type of Government: Royal Empire/ Parliamentary

Type of Law System: Surveillance society.

Population: 12.63 million

Elevation: Mount William 347,903 meters
Grace Beach 0 meters

Geography: Hilly. Sporadically paved. Mostly farmland outside of the capital city of Camelot. Lake Stephen is being fed by Merlot river. The whole west side of the continent has a deep reef with massive crashing waves. The only ways to enter island via ocean is the northeast or southeast sides of the continent.

Most Common Tree: Stomp Wood

Sovereignty is a mix of the descendants of Europe, mainly those that were spread out on the other carriers. The Irish, Spanish and French. British leftovers as well. All decided once they landed here, that they'd get together and try to resurrect the old ways of living. A new Europe. But they gave the land a name to let the new world know what they wanted for their future. The leadership of Sovereignty is isolationist. They are determined to keep their history alive. So they have been restructuring Sovereignty to have the exact borders of Europe and dimensions as they were on Earth.

The current leader of the continent is a descendant of one of the offshoots of the British royal family. They decided to go to a royal system after it was discovered that two of their citizens shared royal genetics. One from the house of Hanover and the other from the abandoned line of Markle. The people chose to honor the British royalty but not the royalty from the other European bloodlines. Those that survived the trip weren't given much thought. But they've gone along with the decisions as long as everyone is being cared for, as long as no one is left behind.

The continent is mostly cultivated and farmed land. They decided to go with a royal system instead of a parliamentary one to make sure that the vision was kept. And with the two competing houses it insured that that vision was upheld, lest they oust one and install the other.

Sovereignty as a continent is small. There appears to be three very large rivers, but it's really two rivers that feed into one which then feeds into a large and immeasurably deep, fresh water lake that they've named Stephens Lake, after King Stephen II, a beloved patriarch from the mid 2300's.

The lowest point of Stephens Lake is on Grace Beach, the only remaining dense forest on the continent. Such a dirty joke the way they structured the land use. They converted the soil quickly and were the first continent to specialize in Earth native foods. Huge market for lettuce, potatoes, carrots and beets. Every human on the planet wanted them. The problem with growing plants native to Earth or Mars in this Vasilian soil, is the high levels of beta-carotene which turns Earth plants which are usually green, orange. And they don't last long.

They've saved their luxury for a multicultural hub that they've dubbed, Camelot. They accomplished this by hollowing the inside of a mountain to build a city within it and all it's connecting mountains. Inside of the mountains contain affixed high-speed transit, large skyscrapers and castles. The roads are paved. It is as if the Alps were hollowed out and they placed the whole of Qatar inside of them.

Camelot is to the south of Stephens Lake, so water is imported via purified pipeline into the city. The main mode of transit across the continent is high speed rail. Sovereignty is a well done continent. I can only hope the Royal leadership continues to make the right choices.

488 Y.A.A.

Continent: Guojia

Capital: New Urga

Leader: Pr. Yuxing Feng. PM. Noy Sayavong.

Type of Government: Parliamentary communists. Rotating responsibilities. Militarism.

Type of Law System: Tribunals.

Population: 18.261 million

Elevation: Mt. Da 94,113 meters
             Li Kai Valley -313 meters

Geography: Continent is split into 6 different countries which meet at a ring of hot springs that surround a volcano. Entire coastline is up to 38 miles of desert sands. There are no major rivers running through the continent. They desalinize or import from nearby freshwater.
     Most Common Tree: Divergent Kai

The outer rim of Guojia is a massive desert that, from the shore, reaches 38 miles inland, all the way around the continent. I didn't know how long it would take to get to civilization, let alone any grass, and it is very disorienting to walk through that much sand with no true idea as to where I am headed. I was simply exploring. Mother once told me she could go a long time without water, but would rather not do so. I have never tried to duplicate her feats during my epoch. But I do know that walking through 38 miles of sand with only a canteen and purifier isn't ideal. I'll definitely never do that again. After passing the sand dunes there is a land of lush orange forests.

The wall of trees seems never-ending. Each tree is wildly shaped with dark gray bark and wide orange leaves. Native animals live around the forests and spend most of their time digging caverns in the ground and in the sides of the hills. No one is privy to why the native life has decided to do this, but the Animal Kingdom is full of caves in mountains and holes in the ground. The thinking is that this planet is full of burrowing animals preparing for hibernation. Two Stomps hasn't told me anything about this practice and I wouldn't dare ask. Not my place. The center-south of the continent contains an active volcanic mountain range. The constant lava flow has flattened the surrounding area and created a brownish black terrain. But on the edge of this flattened land is an ash border against a huge lava wall between the end of the forest and the beginning of the lava. There, sits civilization.

    The hardest or most difficult thing about navigating Guojia is dealing with the borders. They were divided into the shape of a pizza, cut in slices. The six groups of people, governments, somehow got the math right. Well initially. There has been a restructuring of the continent in my last decade here. Now it's a weird puzzle. The area is the same, but their mutually agreed upon constitution forbids any one government/nation from having any more land than another. They made sure that every nation would have no more or no less land than the other nations that make up Guojia. So there are exchanges.
The continent is divided evenly but with weird borders. The history of these people is complex. The main government is based on the ideal of socialism, but not as it was on Earth. They have a rotating government model. The only real consistency is in their approach in dealing with the animals and with other humans. The six nations are China, Mongolia, Laos, Vietnam, Cuba, and Indonesia. On Mars they were a tense alliance that grew amicable, now they have grown much closer in the past few centuries, aided by the trip to this world. More peaceful. However, they still believe in nationalism. Also, each of the nations that share this continent agreed to let the native animals exist here as long as they didn't mind staying on with the humans. Two Stomps gave his blessing.

The government currently is under the leadership of President Yu Xing Feng and a Prime Minister Noy Sayavong. The six nations that make up this land mass have created the semblance of stability. But it has the potential to crumble. The wrong leadership or a corruption of ideals will likely happen and could lead to their downfall. I've found that some of the people of Chinese ancestry are overly invested in their heritage. Maintaining their heritage at all costs may be the flint that ignites the gunpowder. And with their alliance to the Animal Kingdom being the strongest, it could lead to a war on a level never seen by human eyes. This has been all the more likely due to the recent assassinations of the top 8 members of Salta De Argentine's government. The assassin left no witnesses and no cameras could find whoever it was. The killer escaped through a ventilation hole that led away from the room that they were holding their meeting. All 8 of the government officials were reported to have been armed with guns, yet they were killed by swords. Only one had time to pull his gun but not enough time to fire. None of this is good. No one has claimed responsibility.

521 Y.A.A.

Continent: Chestnyy

Capital: Kazangrad

Leader: Soshanna Saushina

Type of Government: Communistic Republic

Type of Law System: Democratic judicial.

Population: 16, 991,736

Elevation: Mount Leningrad – 79,198 meters
　　　　　　　Tovar Beach - -1002 meters

Geography: Mostly cold. Connected to cold animal kingdom through land bridge made of ice. Could be a glacier. Deep, cavernous ocean immediately off the shore makes swimming impossible for humans. Below Hevioso debri moon.
　　　　　　Most Common Tree: Harse Grain Tree

There is a way to Chestnyy that makes me hope that humanity can be this way forever. The people on this continent are caring, humble. They want peace and harmony. They don't strive for prosperity, aren't guided by greed. For them to be this kind and generous is a credit to their leadership. It also has led me to believe that they are hiding something or hiding from something. That maybe they know something the rest of us do not.

I arrived on Chestnyy after over 30 years of wandering around New Urga. The population of Guojia has more than doubled in my time on their continent, so I felt it necessary to move on, especially with the infighting going on in the government. Chestnyy is different. Their government is more complex, yet reasonable. That is desirable for what comes next, for what must come. I sense war is coming due to the assassinations worldwide of any political figure advocating aggressiveness towards another nation. Historically, that never goes well.

Chestnyy is surrounded by deep, turbulent waters which stretch all around the continent. The top of the world, which is the middle of the continent, is dense with cold orange forests, the northern most point covered in ice and darkness. Slivers of light from the bright giant pierce the darkness periodically. The darkness is because of Hevioso, the tidally locked moon directly overhead. There is also a thin land bridge that separates Chestnyy and the Northern Animal Kingdom. This bridge, I've seen, is clear. Like the clearest glass. You can see the water and animals moving beneath it. Shark like animals with tentacles like octopuses. The fish all have tendrils. Any ocean animal without tentacles or tendrils that ventures too close to the surface, does so because they no longer have tentacles due to age or battle and were ready to be food. Such was the totality of the rule of Two-Stomps and his lineage that every creature knew when to become food. And no time before. I've now seen what a true ruler and their reach could be.

The humans of Chestnyy have built a society, one with nature. They live in tree homes. Peacefully. The earth animals have lived in peace with the native animals. Learning from them. Falling in line. Picking up behaviors. The Earth animals appear to be getting smarter. Verbal. Scientists think its a reaction to the water and vegetation. There are no active volcanoes on Chestnyy, no geysers. The most identifying feature of Chestnyy is what colonizers called The Gorge. A mountain range that was struck by the monstrous asteroid that became Evergreen many years before humans arrived, which sent chunks into space creating the moon, Hevioso and a hole below in that range. The crater resembles a sideways Grand Canyon of Earth. And it is in that chasm that the capital city of Kazangrad was built. The soil of the city is covered in aluminum sulfide, which is a nightmare, but at least due to the flocculation, the grass is green in the crater, making it the most Earth-like city on this planet. The plants are all monoecious here. Not so much on most of the rest of the planet.

746 Y.A.A.

Continent: Afriq

Capital: Cagoria

Leader: Queen Earth of Cagoria

Type of Government: Monarchy

Type of Law System: Peacetime/Common

Population: 26.39 Million

Elevation: South Zion Mountain Range 398,717 meters
The Mandela Cavern - -2700 meters

Geography: A mix of plains, deserts and forests. Two massive and deep lakes. The Queendom is breathtakingly simple in design. The various provinces all obey the rule of the queen. Worlds largest land locked lake in the eastern part of the continent.

Most Common Tree: Aira Ydolem

After over 200 years on Chestnyy, I had to move on. I had explored and even isolated myself enough there. I feel that I also failed to act at the fighting between the different nations, continents. Some of which were leveraging their own animal alliances against each other, which was easier to do with the death of Two-Stomps, having gave himself to the swamp dinosaurs as a means of honoring his own rule. The new leader of the Animal Kingdom is a silicon based, reptile- like creature. One that the subjects of his new kingdom call him, Hard Mouth. He gained the throne by virtue of support by a majority of the kingdom. The ocean creatures also approved his rule. Because Hard-Mouth is silica based, his throne room isn't in the mountain caves like Two-Stomps, it is at the northern point where the volcanoes and lava cliffs are. He is basically a rock monitor lizard that lives inside a lava cavern. My concern is that he is being manipulated by the humans trying to gain his support.

The Queendom of Afriq has been most notable in sending envoys to try and build an alliance, one more favorable than they had with Two-Stomps. Over the 700 plus years of Two-Stomps rule, Afriq made their way to the bargaining table only a handful of times. Instead, choosing to go it alone. They released all of the earth / martian animals on the continents ecosystem. Animals that they had cooped up in their ship for centuries, were left to run roughshod on whatever may be. Panthers, deer, pigs, crocodiles and countless species of reptiles both poisonous and not. How they kept them alive on the ships so long, or even got them acclimated to this planet, I will never quite understand. But they did it. Those animals that they let run free were supposed to be a signal to Two-Stomps that they were peaceful. And when that didn't curry favor with the Animal Kingdom, the people of Afriq became who the people of Earth were before it went downhill fast. Breeding the animals, in order to increase their numbers to feed the populace. I was informed by locals and many of the other leaders, that Afriq had only ever been under the rule of a Queen. The people that live here prefer it that way.

The here is otherwise majestic. The Queendom allowed the artificial intelligence free reign in designing and building the structures all across the continent. The computer engineers seem to have made the corrections to insure that what happened in the original programs on Mars, never happens here. What this has done is made it so that the AI has mined this land for minerals and ore suitable to build for humans. They've built a power grid that utilizes Tesla coils and many more recent technologies. The AI also found new elements while mining. Combined elements and original. The Queendom thus had a large head start on all of the other nations that came after them, most of which decided against using AI in fear of reigniting the horde. So, they bounded ahead technologically. And structurally.

There is so much to learn about this continent besides the history of the people that live here now. The geography is astounding. Lake Sahara is the biggest internal body of water on this or any continent and no one has found its maximum depth yet. No human vessel has made it deep enough thus far and no ocean creature that was released by any of the ships from their aquariums have rebounded. The animals, mammals and reptiles originally from Earth, have flourished here. In the early years they moved much slower due to the gravity, but they got from here to there faster than humans. The hierarchy is the same, from rat to rabbit to puma. Their scientists say that they have gotten faster with every generation, which is terrifying.

Earth birds only fly short distances, they mostly stay on the ships or in aviaries in Afriq, reluctant to exert themselves or become food for the larger flying natives like the Prae. They've all become colorful chickens. The rest of the continent is a confluence of rivers, sporadic forests and mountains that scrape the atmosphere at the eastern edge.

The buildings that were designed by the AI all resemble the drawings from those colorful rhyming books meant to teach children to read and use their imaginations. AI determined that the way the gravitational pull and alternative weather structure occurred that the buildings and even the homes would benefit from not being the rectangles or squares of our past, but either pyramids, domes or oblong formations.

    The weather on Afriq holds true. All of the continents and nations located on the equator of this world are lucky enough to maintain a steady temperature and weather system. Feels like spring all the time. Because of this, the clothing that the people wear ranges from very loose and modest to barely there. On Afriq, the people's clothing is spacious and loose. This is a very interesting place.

908 Y.A.A.

Continent: Eden

Capital: Genesis

Leader: Reverend Benito McIlvane

Type of Government: Parliamentary Dictatorship

Type of Law System: Catholic doctrine.

Population: 19.82 Million

Elevation: Mount William – 477,377 meters
Sinai Beach – -28 meters

Geography: Cities are largely walled or domed. Towns resemble dark ages Earth paintings. Castles of stone and homes of mud. The capital, Genesis, is a glass metropolis under a retractable dome in the middle of a desert. The biggest river, Sinai, is dark, yet clear and runs in, through and out of the city. Waterfalls dominate the land down to a volcano.

Most Common Tree: Synthase Elm

I have made my way to Eden "the glass continent". After 150 earth years on Afriq, I knew it was time to move on and explore more. I had to cross the Zulu mountain range to get off of Afriq, which is frigid. Very cold. From there I had to catch a dingy across weird water and around loose, floating islands. There are no air strips or public helipads on Eden. The only way anyone is allowed on the continent is by chancing what they call the Mouth of God. The Mouth is a two mile wide opening leading to a waterfall between a mountain range. Below the waterfalls are rapids that seem beyond class 3. After a few miles, the river splits off into two large rivers, which then begin to split off into smaller and safer rivers across the continent. One of the rivers, however, leads to another waterfall right into the mouth of a large lava pool. So, depending on which route you take on the initial fork on the Mouth of God, you can either lead yourself to a quiet ride down many different and safe rivers, or into a fiery pit. I do not envy the first people to have found this out.

The borders of Eden, are either a series of hollowed out mountain ranges converted to domes in the north and west ends just like the ones in Sovereignty, or glass domes on barren lands of the east. It is unclear if humans started hollowing out hills and mountains or just did what the animals did to the extreme. The southernmost border, which is in the cold uninhabitable zone is a series of glacial hot geysers. In the southern area, just south of the lava bed, is a lush forest of gigantic trees that is continuously covered in ash. The cities of Eden are all villages with different sects of the Christian/Catholic religion in charge. All of the different sects inhabit their own villages across this gigantic continent. I've even seen Mennonites and snake handlers on my travels. It is a weird blast from the past to see these beliefs somehow survived the expanse of space to continue even here. The capital is a glass city named Genesis that they built over the top of the river they named Mary. Located in the southeastern area, this was the first location in which they landed when trying to find a place to settle. There are no local animals, just earth animals. I have learned that this was the first nation to immediately relocate every native animal or kill them if they resisted, drawing permanent ire from the Animal Kingdom.

My purpose on Eden is to facilitate the meeting between Eden's new leader, Reverend McIlvane and Guojia's newly appointed leader, Qiuhua Ge. Qiuhua asked me, since I was on my way here anyway, to go and learn as much as I could about the Reverend, as both are just taking their oaths of leadership. She wanted to see if he was the kind of man that could be reasoned with. I don't think that he is. I told her as much. Yet, she believes that his politeness over a communication was more than gentlemanly posturing. He is a man of gargantuan piety and I don't think he can be trusted to do anything but follow the rulings of his lands religion under advice of the second in command, Pope Evangeline the Second. I have requested an audience with his staff next month with the hope of meeting him soon. I'll send a communication back to her and let whatever happens, happen.

928 Y.A.A.

Continent: Ayat

Capital: Ibrahim City

Leader: Omar Shakir Lemo

Type of Government: Parliamentary dictatorship

Type of Law System: Non-invasive religious adherence.

Population: 22.1 Million

Elevation: Mount Sabah 978,811 meters
 Nur -10

Geography: Shores are at least 10 meters above ocean level. Entire land is elevated. Rivers are not irrigated but are used. Cold northern area filled with waterfalls that feed into both freshwater rivers. Various mountain ranges that reach untold heights.
 Most Common Tree: Divergent Kai

I left Eden as quickly as I possibly could. To date, it is the shortest amount of time I've spent on a continent. I never plan on going back, at least until they evolve past their current ideologies. Reverend McIlvane did what I told President Ge that he would do. He tempted her, used her standing and propped himself up to gain traction for Eden in Guojia. This led to her impeachment and imprisonment. Then, McIlvane denied any wrongdoing and claimed it was the will of god that she was imprisoned. If I had the will, or a warriors heart, I'd do what should be done to McIlvane.

Ayat has, in the last 900 years since it was settled, gave a level of mystery and fear to everyone not on Ayat. I've been wandering around the mountains to the north for a good 6 years now, and the people I've encountered here in the villages and cities are peaceful, smiling and ultimately respectful. There is no savagery or hateful propaganda against other nations or ethnicities. Just people observing their religion and living. Thriving. Now, are the rules strict? Yes. But they are absolutely livable. All are equal and allowed to fulfill the same roles in life and job. Their leadership is indeed a mystery. A woman is in charge of ministry. She's a fundamentalist and is rumored to be in possession of a very strategic mind. The seemingly arcane laws and rules she has Ayat following that absolutely terrify those that aren't citizens, mostly deal with the laws men must follow. They follow the teachings of Islam and those men who do not honor one of those teachings, or in a phrase, protect women, are dealt with harshly.

Women currently outnumber men on Ayat to the tune of 6.1 to 1. The reason for this is because of the fighting against the horde all those years ago. People of the Muslim faith, whatever nationality they identified as, sent all of their men, young and old, to fight against the horde so that the women and children could escape Mars on the world carriers. They protected women. Of the three abrahamic religions, only the Muslims did so. The other two branches made excuses as to why they couldn't risk that many men. Mostly the men making themselves indispensable. Such cowardice is remembered even today, which is why they are still isolated and not trusted. When asked about the division, the locals say that it isn't persecution if it is deserved. They are, even still, deserving of this forced recompense. The Muslims lost all of their adult men to the fight, what was left were the women to teach the children and lead on the ships. The responsibility to pass on the faith to the young and raise them fell to women. And when they settled here, the women were in charge. The women made sure that they all were respected and their independence honored like they had been deprived of previously. The faith that they now have as the true representation of Islam, is a continuation of what was. It is their idea of the evolution of the prophet's message. It is why they named their nation, Ayat. To continue the story of life.

South of these mountaintops, are the two rivers that meet to create one river that runs the length of Ayat. Their names are Hagar and Ibrahim, with the one singular river spawned being named Ishmael. The sentiment is beautiful. Every city is built to be extravagant but humble along the length of the Ishmael river. They do not irrigate and change the course of the waterways like other continents have done, they have instead decided to build feeder pipes to reach those that don't have access to the rivers. All of this was done to continue the living metaphor under the current government led by Inaya Al Riah. Daughter of Nora Al Riah. The Riah bloodline has been involved with politics for a long time here on Ayat and are a long line of teachers and clerics.

The rules and laws that are feared, the ones that make people refer to them as savages or uncivilized have to do with a simple premise. Failure to protect women. If you refuse to protect women or are someone that causes harm to women then you cannot be devout and they treat those that fail, accordingly. As far back as I have learned, this began in 23YAA with the first female cleric to claim power here in Ayat. Her ruthless regime scared much of the men away that were expecting to be powerful clerics on a new planet. As it were explained to me, the men that were found to not be devout, were mated with, then sent to the ceremony of death. The condemned are given the chance to select three female warriors, military, to mate with. 30 years or older. Those three women, for one month all mate with him continuously. Once they are all confirmed pregnant, they team up to fight him in combat. Three on one. The women in this military, are mythical. Highly trained. Stuff seen in the films of old from Earth. Simply fighting one unarmed and untrained man, one on one, usually leads to death for that man. Three on one is overkill. If the man somehow wins, he is instead castrated and exiled to a living zoo. Because any man willing to show aggression towards a pregnant woman, is not worthy of being a part of civilization. They are to be exiled and made to perform dua until they die. They are never seen again. Protect women indeed.

971 Y.A.A.

Continent: Judea & Power grid

Capital: Jerusalem

Leader: Yael Cohen

Type of Government: Military Republic

Type of Law System: Tribunal

Population: 11,018,396

Elevation: North Ice Wall -17,003 feet
Isiah Canyon – 203 meters.

Geography: Ice wall surrounds most of the continent. They have built caves into the cliff faces and have military outposts in those caves. There are multiple geothermal hot spots. Springs. Militaristic nation.

Most Common Tree: Big Hollow

I accepted an invitation to have dinner with a friend. He is an ambassador that I met while on Eden as he studied the volcanoes, but he lives on Judea. He hasn't seen me in thirty years and has no idea about my condition. He was in his early twenties at the time of our first encounter and we have kept in touch over time by using digital communications. While his face has changed and aged, mine has not. I still look like I did when I turned twenty two and my aging paused. Here are the facts that I know about Judea.

They are or were separatists. Gentiles aren't typically allowed unless accompanied by a host or host family. The only way to live here is to be a descendant of Jews that lived on Earth. So Haredi, Dati, Masorti and Hiloni. Or more specifically, Israelis, Orthodox and well, everyone else. They have become, as a people, very much addicted to war and paranoia. They initially fought a fruitless 30 year war with Ayat just for the land they were already living on. They thought that the women of Ayat were trying to keep the skirmishes of the distant Earth past going and were not going to just let them live. It took 30 years because there weren't any intercontinental ballistic missiles or silos. The people of Judea built a sizable navy while Ayat focused on defending its borders with weaponry and shielding. They also built defensive boats and a submarine, but launched nothing because they didn't want to intrude upon the waters of a planet they were guests on. They were assured at the time by Two-Stomps that any boats in the oceans, beyond the shores that were allotted to them, would not be permitted. Ayat had no other allies and Judea had allied itself with Eden. Once it was found that Eden and Judea had become allies and were building power plants and other energy sources on the nearby island to Judea, in order to have the upper hand on Ayat, several of the more "non-religious" nations got involved both physically and diplomatically to drive Judea back to their land. When shame didn't work, they flew planes filled with supplies for Ayat. And when that wasn't a deterrent, they joined Ayat's ranks. 3 years after that, the war ended. The details of which are murky but it is said that someone in Judea, one of the citizens, assassinated half of the military commanders and government level war mongers and made it known that if they continued the war, that the other half would be soon to follow. Judea then built their natural ice wall up to surround almost the entire continent over the span of 300 years and secluded themselves after that. No one knows what is going on except the people that have been allowed to visit. They have assigned their entire navy to surround the continent. I was allowed to enter the continent through the tunnels. The current president is Orthodox. Hard-liner, but was also the most permissive of all the candidates he was running against. He is on the 8th year of his 10 year term.

Judea itself is very beautiful outside of its history. Lots of 3 story buildings. Few skyscrapers. Roads, freeways and mile wide trees. The trees are a wonder. The tunnels follow the roots of all the trees and connect everything for thousands of miles under various portions of the land all the way out to the shores. The capital city is massive and can only be accessed through a cave which goes underground. But it is also hard to tell where it is exactly due to the tunnels. My friend tells me that they built the capital underground in the roots to protect against a nuclear war that was sure to happen. The border to the land bridge which connects the neighboring continent that they've got all of their energy resources and research being built on is a mystery to me. I wasn't allowed to see the energy plants, but I'm told there are plenty of things inspired by the 25th century, Earth inventor, Vusterdinho.

998 Y.A.A.

Continent: The Isle

Capital: None

Leader: None

Type of Government: None

Type of Law System: None

Population: Myself

Elevation: 2190 meters at its highest point.
        -17 meters on most of the land (flooded)

Geography: Average temperature on the isle is 99F. Most of the island/continent is underwater most of the year. Flatlands. Desert. Volcano. Swamplands. Waterfalls and rivers that flood. Humans couldn't take the heat above 68F comfortably due to time on Mars and space at fixed temperatures.
        Most Common Tree: Great Yanse
    Moments have been replaying in my mind. I've had plenty of

time for them to do so as I sit on this mountain ledge on The Isle. The Isle is a floating continent that sinks and later rises unpredictably. When it sinks, it submerges. The only thing that remains above the water is the mountain range and the Great Yanse tree. When the continent rises, it dries out and burns the oceanic life that grows on it while the land is submerged for a while until the waves put out the fires. The surface temperature of the sands, reach 81 degrees Celsius and is completely humid with steam burning off the sands for 4 weeks straight once it rises. No one has figured out why it continues to rise before falling again. This place is what I imagine an uninhabited Atlantis would have been. With the only anomaly being the active volcano on the island located on the southern edge.

The history of this land is tragic of course. Originally there was a group that settled in the southern parts of the land. It was said to be lush and covered in plant life. After a year and a half, just as fall was about to approach with the discoloration of the plants and the fleeing of the flying animals, the continent had a series of earthquakes and began to sink. Tidal waves more massive than anything these humans had seen up until that point in their lives, began cascading across every part of the settlements. Most of the people escaped in time but there was catastrophic loss of property and life that wasn't seen again until Evergreen. They tried to investigate how much of the continent sank, but couldn't find the rest of the continent until it got to the mountains. That's when they came to the horrific realization that everything was gone.

The mountain range surrounding my spot currently, is just to the north of this planets equator. The planet rotates fast for its size, but takes a long time to rotate once. A full planetary rotation here is 124 hours. Or 5 Earth-like days and 4 hours. The Vasilian year is about 9 Earth years. That's how long it takes to rotate around the bright giant. The mountain range is in the middle of the continent, so whenever it sinks there is no way out, because of the tidal waves and lack of structures. This has left me without much to do except dream.

The continent dropped two months ago and the tsunamis stopped 70 hours ago, which has given me free time. I've been thinking about my mother and her writings. When my sister was born, I was 6 or 7 years old. I could hear mom laughing in the delivery room. I sat next to Grandma, dad's mother, and she told me that my mother laughed through my birth as well. The pain of childbirth now seems unholy and Mom laughed through it. That was 1600 years ago. When mother told me about our gift, our immortality, I knew immediately that she was telling the truth. Not because I felt it, because I was quite mortal at the time, but because the stories she told us about the past came from her heart. She wanted me to be safe until I was able to be free. She said her children, the others that are long gone, were trained as warriors because that was what she knew. Fighting. But me, she wanted me to survive. Our planet was making sure that our entire species died. When they dropped me off at the shuttle site, I remember my sister's crying through their masks. My father remained stoic. Mother walked me to the gate, gave me a hug and told me to stay alive long enough to see her again. Then she walked back and stood with everyone else, their heads held high. I wish I knew how she was doing. How all of them did. If father finished the bunker or if my sisters made it to immortality. If not, what has mom been doing. Is she traveling? Learning? Has the planet rebounded. Is Earth's air still poison? In time I hope to find a way to be able to go back and get her. When humanity catches up to where it's imagination is technologically.

And as always. the other person going through my mind, is her. Over a thousand years and I haven't found anyone who made me want to love again. Not like her. I don't know if that is why I'm traveling. Why I haven't just stayed in one place forever. Become part of a society. Help build it. Found a home. I look at the images I have of her. The pictures. And I can still remember how I took them and where we were. I can smell her hair's scent and see the water trickling from her chin to her clavicles and onto her blanket. I can hear her toes sliding along the floor whenever she just finished showering. Her golden brown complexion dimly lit by the sun's red glow drifting between clouds and into the dark blue shelter. I just wish I had more time with her. The joy we could have experienced. I wonder how she would have reacted to my agelessness. Would we have wanted children and would those children have survived with me to make it to this planet. Would she have loved me forever as I have her?

1076 Y.A.A.

Continent: Cold Animal Kingdom

Capital: None

Leader: Ooer The Large

Type of Government: Strongest rules/Kratocracy

Type of Law System: Everyone for themselves

Population: 900 humans (give or take)

Elevation: Mountain. 391,099 meters
        The Caverns of Ooer -3200 meters

Geography: Southern shore is a desert, inside of that area is a forest. Then ice. The further north you get the more violent the animals and terrain are. Animals are all contenders to be Apex. Moon (Hevioso) is tidally locked overhead and 210,000km away.
        Most Common Tree: Stomp Wood

The only thing I am currently is grateful. After being stuck on The Isle for close to 90 years, one of the sea animals, an AWF, saw me and pitied me enough to get me off of my mountain. I rode on his back passed all of my failed rafts. The Isle is a large place. I still don't know what causes it to sink and rise, but I know the signs now. And it's best to stay off The Isle until you do. The AWF took me to the shores of a place I was warned to avoid by Two-Stomps. Korwl, the Cold Animal Kingdom. He told me that those monsters were rogue. Primitive. Which is saying a lot because they seemed slightly primitive themselves. Two-Stomps told me that the creatures that live there didn't bow to his rule. This is a land filled with the offspring of his challengers. Beasts that didn't respect his orders or strength. They were said to be more into individualism than the good of the collective. Seems downright human. There are actually humans living on the edges of the land but just out of reach of the turbulent waters caused by the moon, that have avoided going too far inland on Korwl. There is a very fragile truce. The settlers released penguins from their zoos after seeing some similar bodied creatures living nearby. And while the indigenous creatures didn't slaughter all of the Earth penguins, they killed many. And they continue to let them get to a certain number before doing so again. Cold and calculating. They treat the penguins like cattle. The penguins are too afraid to get in the water for very long because of the predators. So they stay on the ice. The Cold Animal Kingdom is cold because of Hevioso, the prison moon directly overhead, about 210,000 kilometers above. The water surrounding this land is volatile because of that moon's proximity. The gravitational harmony causes the tide to rush through a canal and into a lake that is itself an earth sized ocean. The shade provided by this relatively small prison moon is tremendous over this continent. Also because of this planet's weird rotation, the shade is widespread.

There is a large orange colored forest that marks the division of humans and creatures, it is the edge of starshine. I passed through the leafless lumps of bark to get to where I hoped to find some creatures with a semblance of civility. What I found instead was a frightening group of highly intelligent, warm blooded, yet lizard like, amphibious animals. Every monstrous creature I have encountered here is both amphibious and fluent in any language the humans of Vasilias speaks. Its like they have the vocal abilities of parakeets. They have learned phrases to say to any human in any language. And even before you speak they can tell what language you use somehow. After being in between the humans and animals for 24 years I was sent a message from a creature known as Ooer The Large. Ooer resembles a very long snake that walks on 8 tendrils. Is as long as a building is tall. Mouth full of jagged teeth and fangs. At the end of it's tail, is a club, not a rattle. Very articulate. The message was "I have shed a skin and I'd like you to take it. When I made it to Ooer, I was gifted with the skin then told to wait. When Ooer saw me, it told me that it could see deep into the stars and that there was a massive ship that just passed around what us humans know to be the star Elnath. That star is light years away, many light years away. Ooer says that their kind can see anything in a straight line and that the ship is moving in this direction. I asked if they had seen the vessel before, and Ooer said no. That they see countless ships pass by and outside of us humans, no one else ever thought to come here. Seems that the air makeup is only agreeable with certain life forms. Lucky us. Then Ooer asked me how old I was, because it has watched me from afar and even followed me from land to land for the last 50,000 lights (days). Now, the days here work differently, with the 4 star system, days last 124 hours and nights last 70 hours. The planet appears striped in night and day but rotates in and out of it. And that is everywhere that there is light and no tidally locked moon. And there are 4 of those. Outside of Hevioso overhead, the other 3 moons that are tidally locked are all over water. Which makes it important to navigate safely because the waters are volatile there and the tidal waves can swell to five hundred feet. I told Ooer that how old I was, was meaningless, because I'm immortal then I asked how long before the vessels get here if they are coming, and I was told that it could be anytime within the next 400 lights. That I need to let humans know, because if this species is like us, that we won't be strong enough to overcome for a very long time. Funny. Humanity has gone from questioning if we were alone in the universe, to knowing we aren't by coming to Vasilias, to soon finding out that we aren't the most advanced life forms intellectually or technologically. I think it might be safe for me to stay here for as long as they'll have me. And maybe I can learn how to look into the galaxy as they do.

1139 Y.A.A.

Continent: Utopia

Capital: Atlantis

Leader: Janus Ryansdotttir & Yosef Oh

Type of Government: Socialist

Type of Law System: Majority rule/Common law

Population: 39.7 million

Elevation: Hitch Mountain 317,917 meters
    Adams Beach -1200 meters (Bottom of Adams Falls)

Geography: Rivers line the land. Stretches across north and south hemisphere. Large waterfalls. Cities built in plains and deserts. Forests left untouched. Southern most tip is cold but warmed by active volcanoes. I was here when the aliens landed.
    Most Common Tree: Tengai Kyodaina

Utopia was originally settled by the atheists and working class people from the ships. That's who lived there the first 30 years after arrival. Other continents/nations largely disregard and despise Utopia. They, the more religious nations, have tried to discredit what they've done here. Which is, build a great nation. When I arrived here 70 years ago after quite some time on Korwl, I was largely ignored and left to my own devices. Traveling around Utopia is difficult, because they don't use anything that resembles an automobile here. Everyone takes the underground zoom tunnels. These tunnels are spread throughout Utopia which easily stretches across the northern and southern hemispheres. The 4 star system makes it so the middle of the continent is an unbearably hot desert. Downright unlivable. 68 degrees Celsius regularly. And that is where they have put their solar panel and satellite array, because there is steady sunshine. The only time this changes is during the three months that it takes the moon, Panacea, to slowly rotate past the continents southern half and eclipses all of the starlight. The whole of Utopia is covered in both freshwater and saltwater rivers as well as dense forests with populated villages of tiny homes and tree-houses. When people get married here, they push their tiny homes together to have a bigger home. It is really quite brilliant.

Utopia, for the most part, cuts itself off from the rest of the planet unless they have allies to trade with. They do have a government, but it is socialist. Truly socialist. They have never had a currency and rely on barter and trade for everything which causes everyone to work on and develop a skill worth trading for. This also makes it so that you have to actually be known to be a leader. You have to spend the time to go around and show you are who people want to represent them.

Crime is punished severely here on Utopia. Their belief is, if you want to get something, have something to trade for it so there should be no reason to steal. Violence of most kinds is frowned upon, drug use of all kinds is accepted, but murder and crimes of a sexual nature are not. Those crimes are punished almost as severely here as they are on Afriq. It is usually dealt with by immediate deportation to Hevioso, regardless of your diplomatic standing. Cameras and drones line the streets of all the cities, rivers and villages so there is virtually no way to get away with those types of crimes. There is an option for those who don't want to go to the moon prison, they can elect to go to the 3 mile, fenced in area in the desert to live in that prison. People that attempt escape from that place are immediately sent to Hevioso upon capture.

The current leadership has been transferring power from Janus Ryansdotttir to Yosef Oh. There's is a 20 year appointment at the top.

Janus won her election by promising more underground construction and she delivered. Yosef won his election by promising more development in the northern mountainous region. He believes that hollowing out one of the mountains will do well to protect the populace in the future. He was formally a diplomat and had traveled to Trade Lands to represent Utopia. While Utopia is despised by the more religious nations, they are respected for their handling of the Evergreen tragedy and taking in refugees, allowing the Wiccans and naturists that survived, land at the southern region of Utopia to live and believe as they want. They and their rule of Hecate are honored as is their sovereignty.

Currently, the world is dealing with what Ooer the Large told me was coming. 46 hours ago, a craft hovered over what was the world power grid and satellite array. A place full of tesla coils, xenon push reverters and super-colliders. The creatures landed there 30 hours later as night approached and when their ship opened, the scientists that lived on the continent stated that they could smell clay. The aliens were large and were said to exhale chlorine. They are said to be bipedal but did not have visible feet or hooves due to their coverings and their upper appendages are very stiff and neon green. The only other distinctive feature is that they have elongated faces. No one has made contact and all humans have abandoned the land in an abundance of caution.

1301 Y.A.A.

Continent: Land of Women and Children (Uchi)

Capital: On'na

Leader: Marada Sittaram, Izumi Mari & Binna Hyum

Type of Government: Socialistic-Democratic

Type of Law System: Common

Population: 29.09 Million

Elevation: Jenny Falls 7100 meters
Base of Jenny Falls -300 meters

Geography: Highest point of the of the continent is a mountain that contains a waterfall. People are instructed not to go near north side of Island because of pheromones from Evergreen island.
Most Common Tree: Giant Hollow

The distance between Utopia and JKI, is the shortest distance of any of the continents on this planet. 12 miles. JKI is known as the Land of Women and Children to the rest of the world, because that is all that is allowed. As soon as any male child reaches 184,000 hours of age, he is asked which continent he wants to be a citizen of. Then that male is transported to that land, never to return. Usually Utopia. Men are only allowed as temporary guests on this land. Short term. And even though they send their adult males away they take pride in valuing their people over their symbolism. And even though they don't value symbolism, they are allied primarily with the Americans. The founder of this nation was a woman named Alexis Del Drogan. She instituted the three tier system that they currently run even today.

The governments of Eden and Judea consider them hedonists. But what I've found is that religion is not part of their discourse, yet they are religiously diverse and they just want to be left alone. JKI is the most technologically advanced nation and provides most of the planet with their technological advancements. They also designed their inventions to not function at all on Eden, Judea and Salta De Argentine. They claim to have evidence of Salta De Argentine's dirty dealings and political assassinations, which is why I'm here.

I am going to be meeting with this continents leaders. The Samshin, which is Korean for 3 goddesses. The current 3 women who decide how the land is governed are Marada Sittaram, Izumi Mara and Binna Hyum. Much like Guojia, the JKI appoints or votes for their leadership to be put into the role of one of the 3 presidents. Equal footing. And only 3, no ties in any vote. A decision must be made with them. They voted to release to me, as the newly appointed ambassador from Utopia, the visual and audio proof as well as written proof of SDA's shady dealings and its allies to bring back to Utopian leadership so that we can choose the right side of the war that is erupting and is soon to be fought. I've seen the evidence and it is conclusive and quite damning. My recommendation will be that we partner with JKI, Chestnyy, U.N.A and both of the Animal Kingdoms against SDA's allies. Namely Eden, Judea, Afriq and Guojia. Unless the other nations believe this evidence, then this war will once again prove that humanity is doomed to kill itself where ever it might go.

As far as the land itself, JKI is, like Utopia, covered in forests with wide trees and a gigantic river that goes through the middle of the continent. Clean, fresh water with huge life forms swimming throughout. The cities are all one or two story buildings as they don't want to be an eyesore to the natural environment. They have domesticated earth animals on the land running loose and being coached to survive by the native animals. The cats have been better at learning the behavior to survive than the dogs. Both of which have grown in size over time. I'm told that a fair amount of the Wiccans and naturists from Evergreen also settled on JKI as a means of being further away from the trauma. Their descendants have intermingled and adapted to JKI's rules over the last 1300 years. This coming war will not be good for anyone and really, I have no idea how it will stop and who is capable of stopping the conflicts.

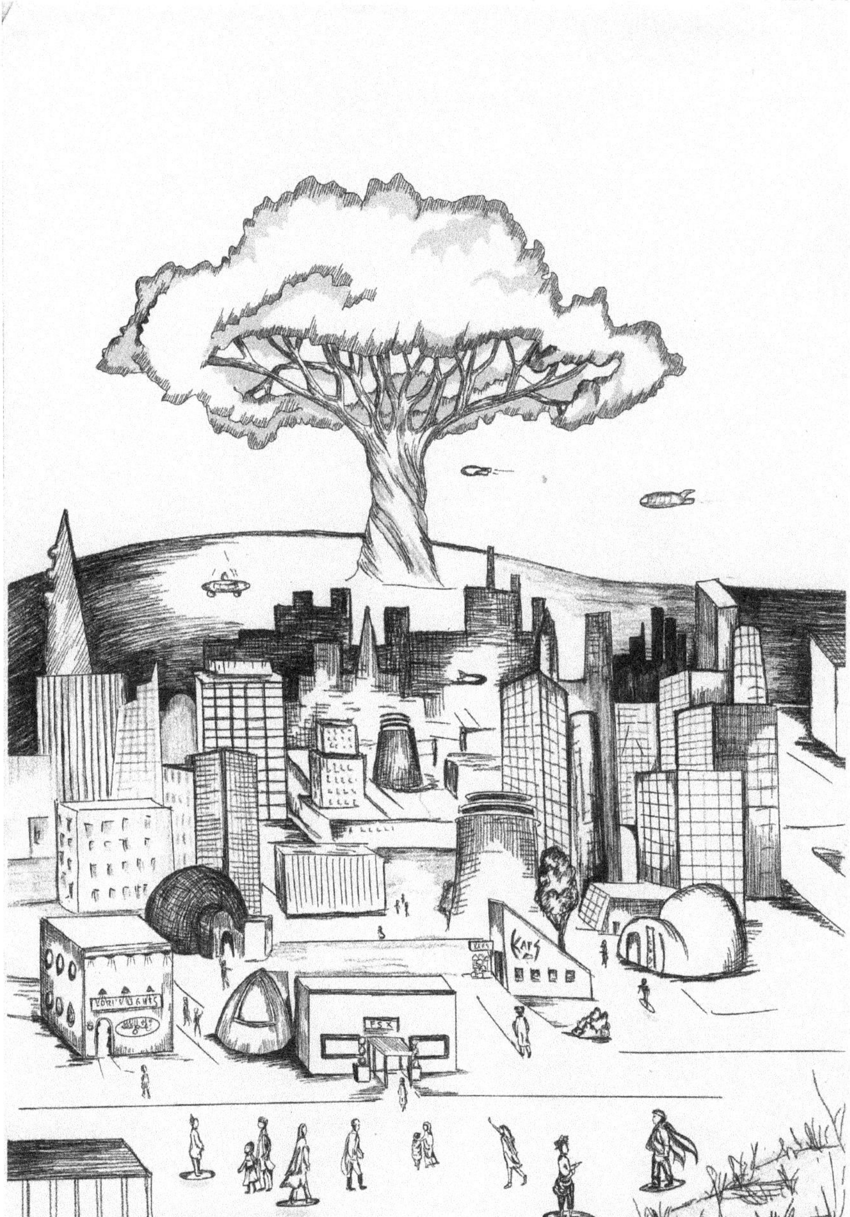
KAFS
FSX

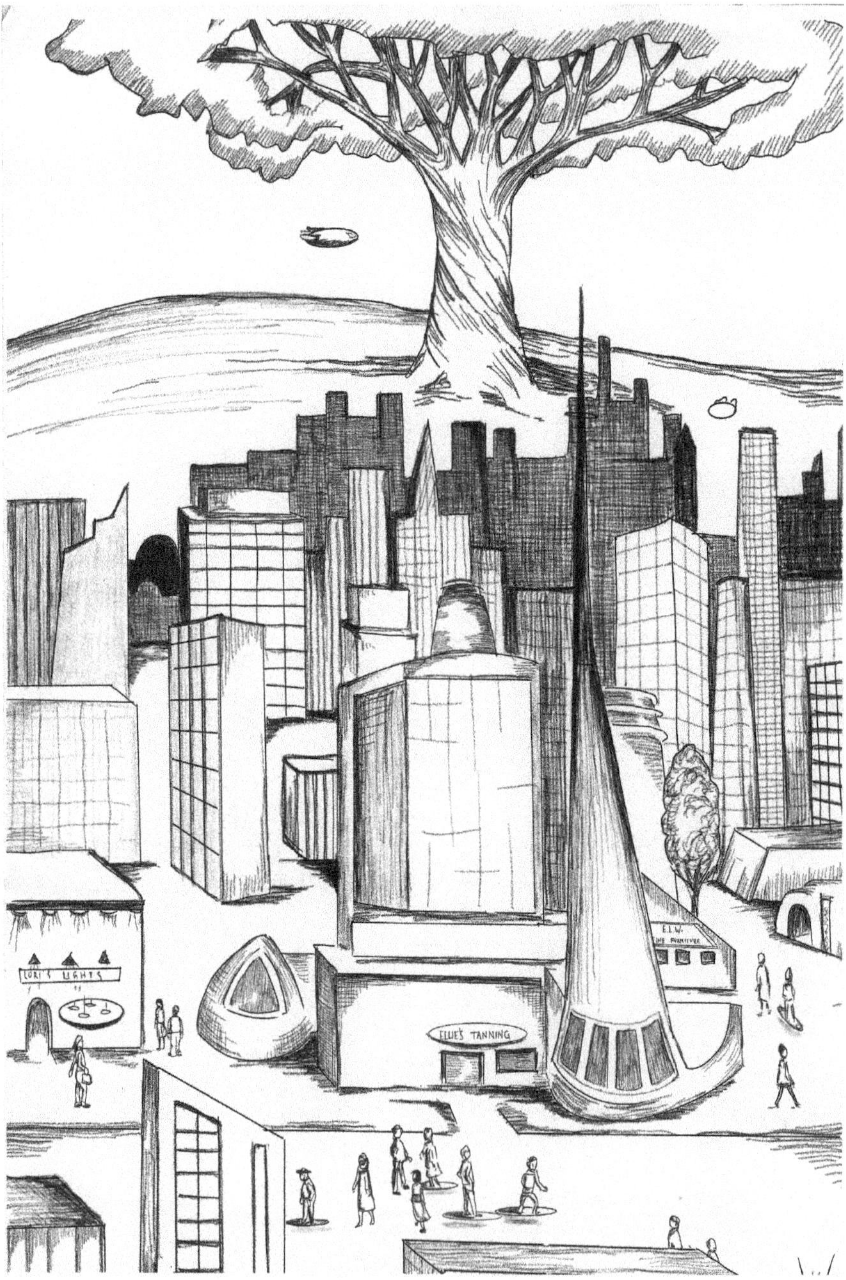
LORI'S LIGHTS
ELLIE'S TANNING
E.L.W.

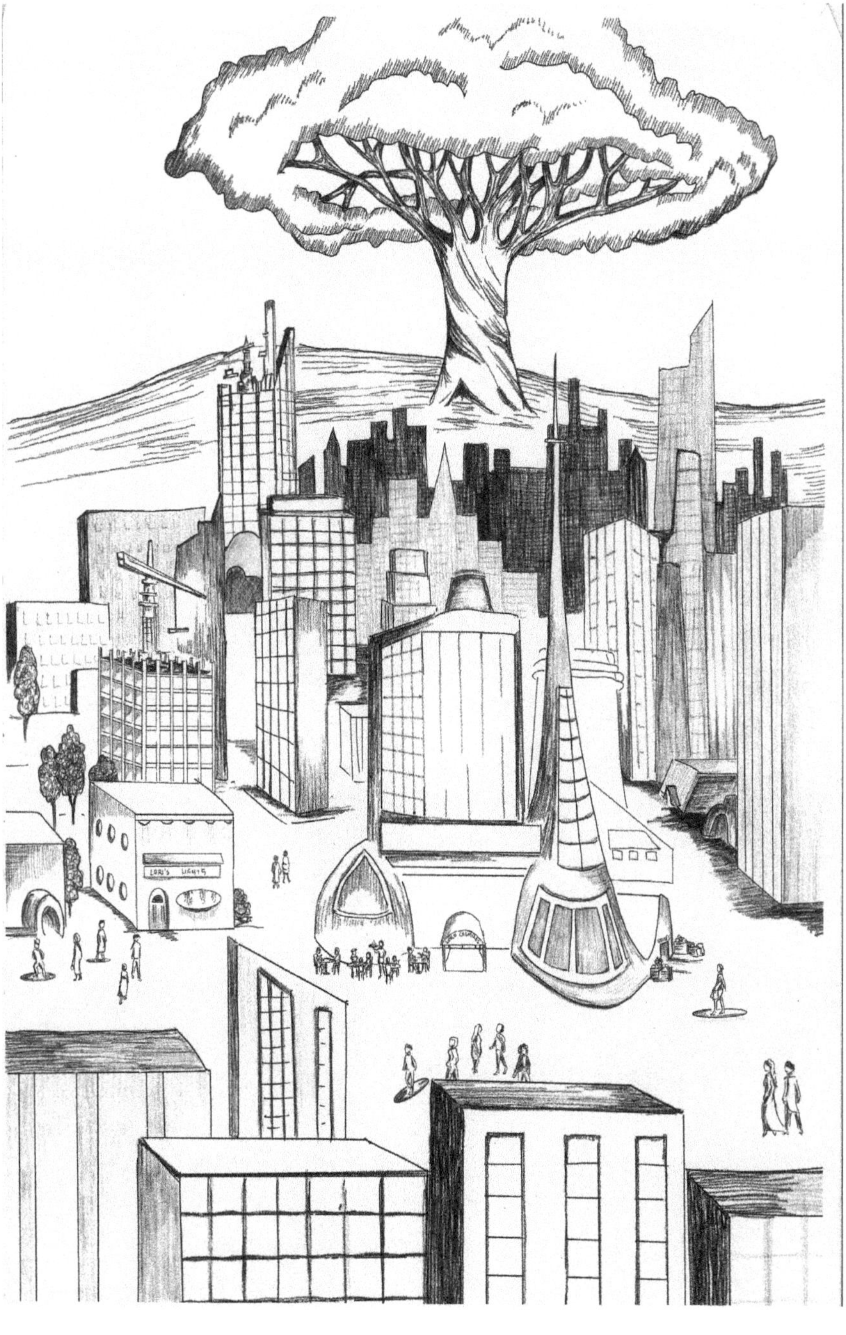

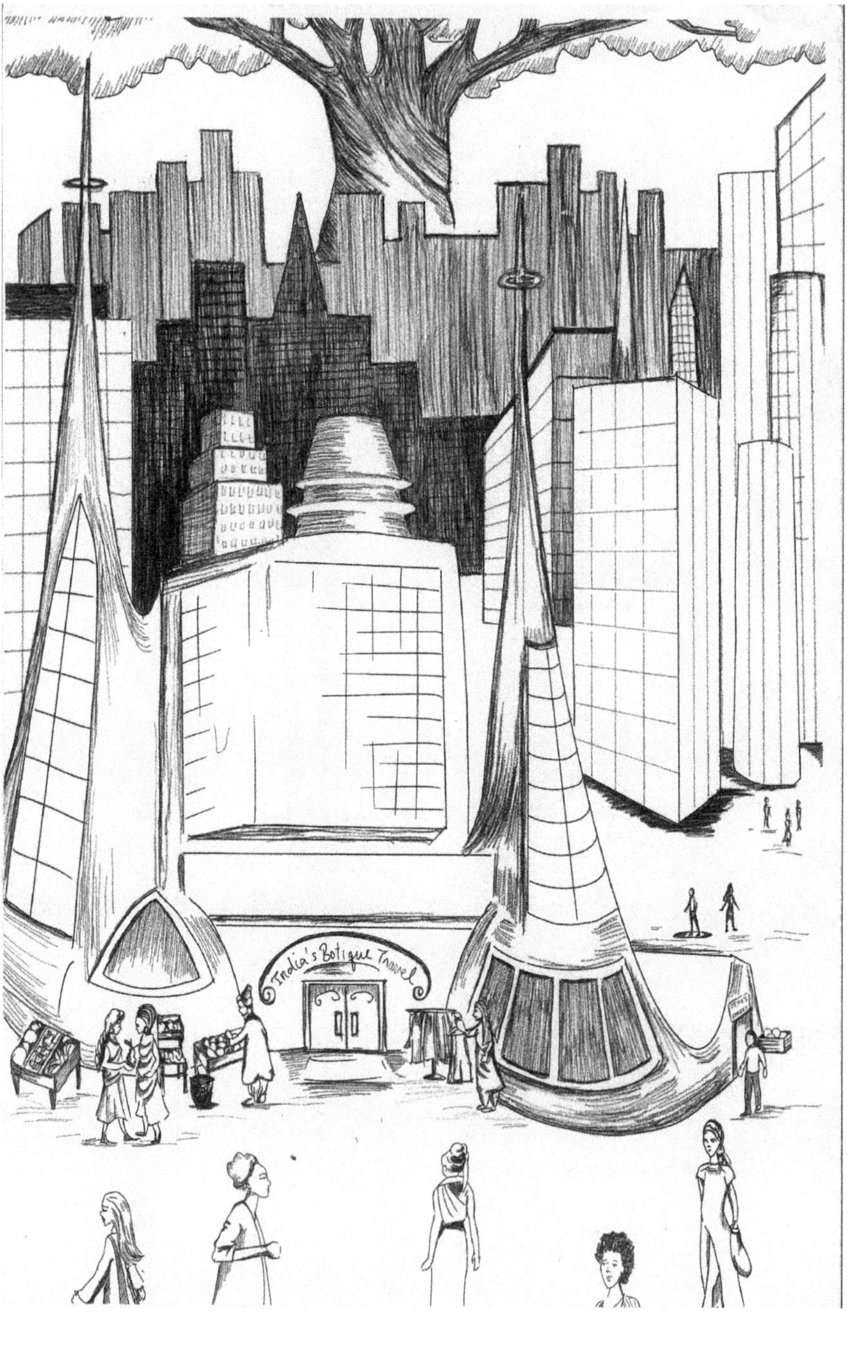
India's Botique Travel

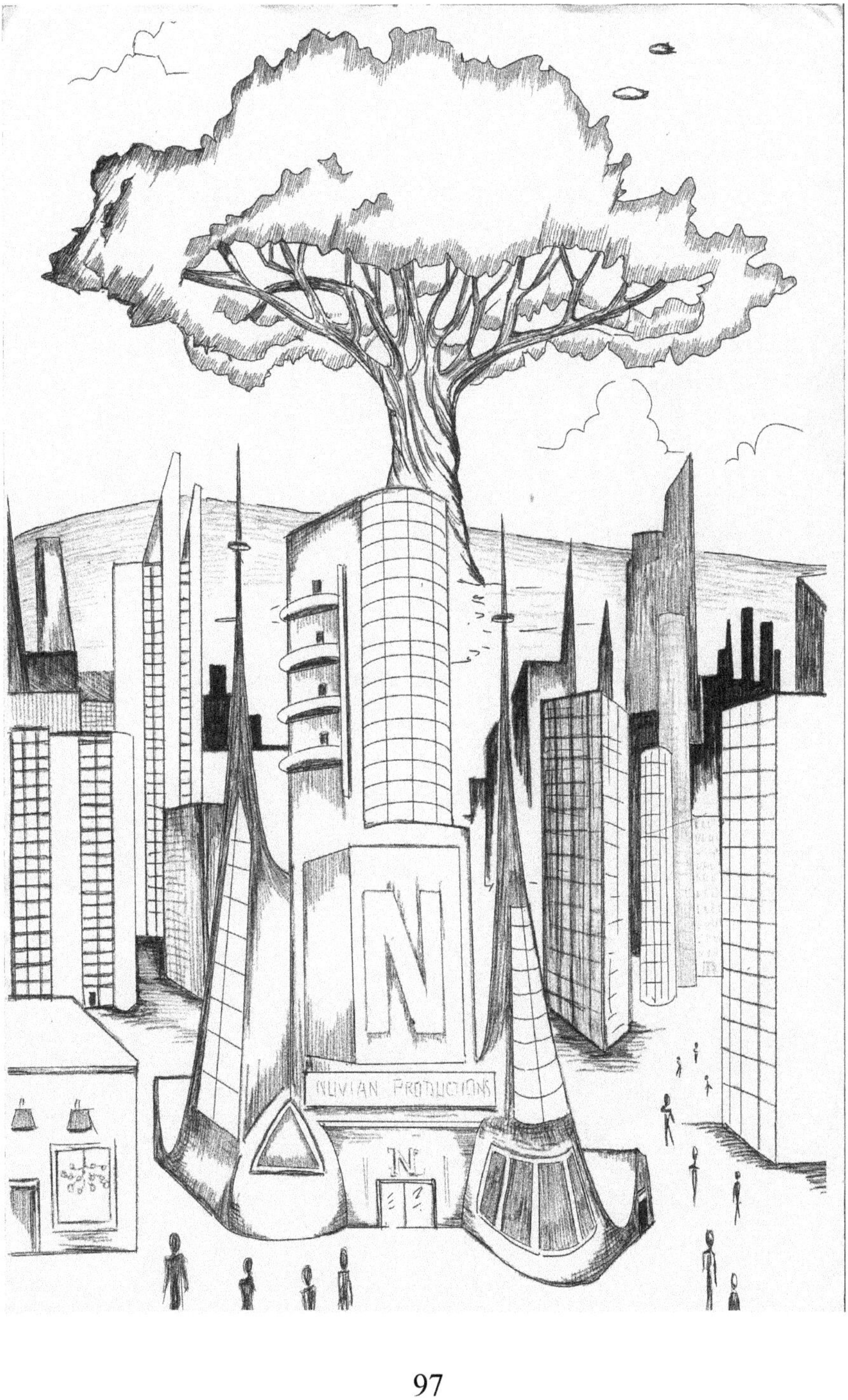
N
NUVIAN PRODUCTIONS
N

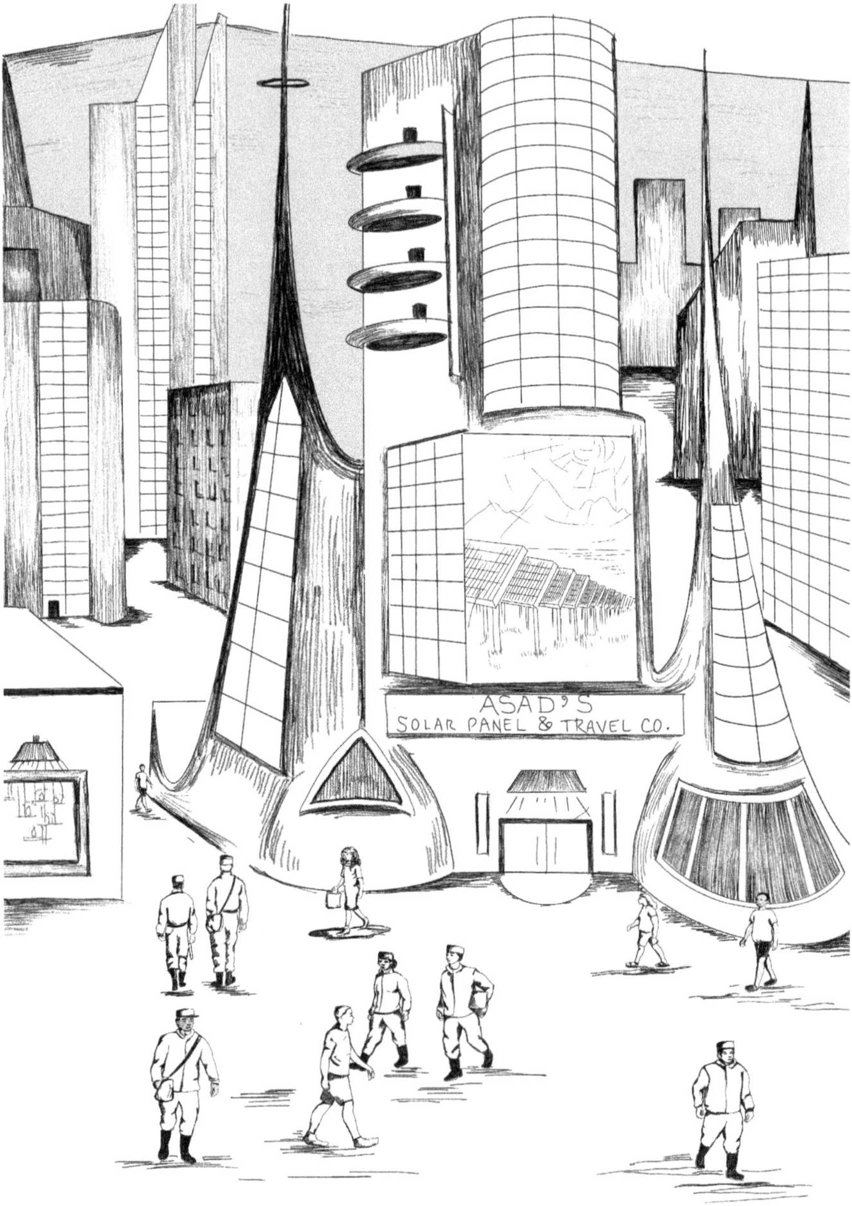
ASAD'S
SOLAR PANEL & TRAVEL CO.

The Evergreen Tragedy.

What I have been able to piece together in the last 1400 human years since I arrived, is that Evergreen was a horrible tragedy that cannot be accurately described. But for this guide to be useful, I have to say something about this event using all of the combined testimonials.

Ooer the Large told me that the forbidden continent came from a planet that was destroyed in the inner rings of the galaxy. Most of this destroyed world was swallowed into the black hole in the center of our galaxy. But remnants big and small spread everywhere. Flying into burning stars and pulsars. Or, crashing into dead planets. That his kind lives in the cold because when they saw what was headed towards this world, they sought audience with their leader and advised migration from the land they were on due to the tidal wave they were sure it would cause by hitting the water. Ooer said that his kind tried to get Two-Stomp's predecessor to listen, but he was too headstrong in his leadership. That the animals were supposed to fall in line and not question the top. And when they openly questioned his leadership, they were made to leave. They were given options, but chose the icy north of the planet because at the time, it wasn't covered in darkness it was a tropical paradise. They tracked the piece of planet that they saw for close to, what had to be 500 Earth years. They didn't know exactly where it would land, just that it would hit this planet in a devastating fashion. And after a long time, they witnessed the first piece careen through the atmosphere and smash into what is now

Chestnyy. The dust and rock shot into the atmosphere and eventually became Hevioso leaving a crater into the side of a mountain range before bouncing into the bottomless lake. The second and much larger piece crashed into the ocean on the side of what is now JKI. It caused waves that crashed over most everything. After it was settled, Ooer said that it didn't take many cycles for the smells to waft all over the planet, which caused any and all animals that were native and had fur to jump in the water. They all started swimming to the new island. Ooer told me that Two-Stomps predecessor had fur like us humans. And he commanded the AWF to give him and any other animal that wanted to go see where the smells were coming from to take them there. And so they did. All of those creatures that went there, never returned. The AWF, told tales so unbelievable that they were shunned, until the Prae flew over and investigated.

And then, much later, human-kind showed up on our vessels. My ship hadn't made it yet, I was still dealing with the horde. According to anyone that has been willing to talk to me about it, as the story went. They all made choices. They argued and divided up who went to which continents. The Naturists and Wiccans chose the land with the weird smell. They assumed it was compost. It was the smallest continent but it was beautiful they say. The colors. The plants. And it didn't matter to these humans that they couldn't find any native animals. They assumed it was where the birds lived. Flying animals like the Prae never seemed to land there. They just hovered overhead watching the humans. The Wiccans released their animals from their ship and the birds chose to stay on top of the carrier. The dogs, cats, pigs and countless other animals ran outside and around. After a few weeks the cats all came running back to the ships. Just the cats. And not a lot of them. The Wiccans and Naturists assumed it was native animals hunting all of the earth animals. The cats refused to leave the ships. They mewed constantly. Some of them were missing pieces of their tails and paws. The humans took up arms and went in search for native predatory animals and found only bloodied pieces of what used to be earth animals. Just pure horror show. For two more months, that is all they found but with plant life sprouting around the pieces. So they returned to trying to make this new land a home. Called it Evergreen.

It took four years before it started again. Children began disappearing. The cats still wouldn't leave the ships and the birds wouldn't land on the ground. Then adults began vanishing looking for their children. They were interviewing people, trying to figure out who the killer was. And while they had suspects, none could be proven to be the killer. Then, during a festival held in the northern part of the continent, the horror started. It was after they lit the bonfire of sage. The land began to quake and, according to legend, you could hear the screams from as far away as Utopia. They flew aircraft and drones over Evergreen and saw screaming bodies, half sticking in the ground. Men. Women. Children. Countless homes and buildings were damaged and sitting half out of the ground as well. The birds, all flying in circles in a panic. Fire raged across the continents grass and plant-life. The photos that the drones took are haunting. People running on bloody limbs trying to make it to the ocean. The ground beneath their feet, dissolving them like acid. Consuming them. In the middle of Evergreen, a hill opened and revealed a large mouth that bellowed out a noise that could be heard by a young Ooer on Korwl. The drone photos show that the mouth was full of dagger like fangs. Utopia sent out distress calls and the only nation to send help was JKI. In the ocean water surrounding Evergreen, was blood. Human and animal blood. JKI and Utopia's watercraft were able to rescue less than 13,000 people. There were 900,000 people that settled there and Evergreen ate almost all of them in one night. Various countries took turns releasing atomic, hydro-atomic, and various nano-weapons on the living continent. They went bomb happy. You could hear Evergreen moan in pain with every missile strike. And that is what united humans and native animals across this planet. That is why the lines of communication opened before I got here. Because the humans did what the native animals could not. They were united in war against one common enemy. And over time they had to find a new enemy when that one was dead. As always, that became each other.

The Moons:

Hevioso. The Prison Moon. Tidally locked over the Cold Animal Kingdom, around 210k miles from the atmosphere. They put you there to exile. There is less gravity, Earth like. One water source that circles the entire moon. Irrigation could spread the water to other parts. It casts a complete jagged shadow over the northern part of the world. Temperatures on surface can be unbearable, but the inner tunnels are livable with the plant life inside. Constant rock showers from Streaffen, the nearby crumbling moon, expand its mass.

Panacea: Moon that orbits the equator of the planet. Surface is covered in an iron like element. Humanity decided to build as many satellites as they could on this moon avoid the trash that was hard to navigate out of Earth's orbit. These range from communication to television to government to surveillance. Gravity on this moon is almost like Earths moon and there is no oxygen. They have built a base meant just for monitoring the satellites for the entire world.

Baoding: Small, tidally locked moon to the north-west of The Animal Kingdom. Causes volatile waters off of the coast. It is made of a soft mine-able metal. They haven't yet figured out what kind of metal this is or what it can be used for. The AI suggests that it can be made to build bigger and stronger ships.

Lughnasad: Called Luna for short. Tidally locked near northern part of Afriq. This is the furthest moon from the planet. 1.4 million kilometers away. The governments are setting up a secondary base to monitor space from there.

Streaffen: Is near Hevioso and is slowly being pulled apart to become part of the north moon.

Voyager: The sulfur moon. Travels in same line as Panacea, but on the southern part of the planet. Is the only moon that can be seen during the day time from south of the equator. Reflects light. Gaseous.

Epilogue:

1,646 years after humanity arrived on Vasilias, nothing has changed in our behaviors. Our order, primates, still behave primitively. Six of the eighteen continents decided to unite to fight a war against 5 other nations. That is how we welcomed our new neighbors, an alien race from a distant part of our galaxy. These aliens have used our resources to learn about humanity. They were not impressed but also not hostile. They peacefully placed all of the human scientific research onto the Trade Lands. The governments decided the trade lands would also be humanities base of research. Subterranean labs were built in the center of the continents hills and the highlands. Far away from the embassy, but not too far. These aliens said to call them Egrendeer. They sent communications that they are an exploratory race, from the outer parts of our galaxy that helps carbon based life forms advance past their intellectual limitations. But that they'll wait until the fighting has ended to do so for us. That was nearly 300 years ago. They remained neutral and watchful the entire time. Patient. The scientists on Utopia speculated that they might be from a level 3 Kardashev civilization because they found a way to convert energy from the lava pools on Vasilias and also started the mining of one of the tidally locked moons.

The war had political prisoners, assassinations and technological warfare. But the humans from the six united continents were only targeting both of the Animal Kingdoms. Not the other mainly human continents. So humans, allied with the native animals, were lost defending those places. There was no storming of beaches, just drone strikes or covert assassinations and the negotiations have been obscenely disrespectful on the side of the aggressors. Their demands ranged from unfettered use of the lands of The Animal Kingdoms, to threats of outright extermination and distribution. Ooer the Large's son, Emar son of Ooer said something at the negotiations so ominous that the allies of the animal nations were put on notice as well. "When the sky soon rises, you'll beg us for mercy." None of us human ambassadors knew what that meant.

It has been 150 years since they found out what that meant. There was an anomaly. A sort of carrington event, but it affected gravity instead of technology. Utopia and the other human allies, were informed by the Animal Kingdom 47 hours before it was to happen to get all of our populations underground or in caves. To do so and ask no questions. I thought that there was going to be an animal assault. Instead, the truth behind all of their tunnel digging and life in caves came to light. There was a flash from the bright giant. The main star. And it triggered a similar reaction from the white dwarf. The closest of the two brown dwarfs happened to be in the path and ignited. Hevioso seemed to suddenly get closer. I was on the cliff face cave watching from the highlands in the Trade Lands. It was majestic for a moment. I felt lighter. I looked out and could see the waves halt and water begin floating. I looked around inside the cave and saw all of the ambassadors allied to the animal kingdom floating, I knew then, what Emar meant and the horror that was about to occur. We didn't expand the ceiling of the cave, it was maybe three meters high. Everyone was pressed against that ceiling, unable to move. I knew that this was going to be happening worldwide. And it was. The people of Eden believed that they were being raptured, as did the people of Judea that weren't in the underground tunnels. Their entire citizenry began going outside to pray and be raptured. Salta De Argentine's citizens, their military, all floated out towards the rising ocean water. The people of Afriq and Chestnyy were able to save a great deal of people by immediately sounding an alarm. It was later revealed that they had some communications a few hours before from the Egrendeer who viewed their nations as valuable scientifically. The worst hit nation was Sovereignty. Their want to live in a manner of being old Earth, lead to half of their citizenship being floated that wasn't working or living in Camelot. This lasted for 21 seconds. The weightlessness. And then the event stopped. And inside the cave we all hit the ground very hard. You could hear the screams from the rest of trade lands. I can only imagine how all of the people felt falling to the ground. Their screams. I don't want to remember their screams. Then the tidal waves began. All over the planet. We were safe where we were, I could see the water rushing by from the cave. We all marveled from inside the safety of the cave. Then we all had the same thoughts. Those poor people who are dying because their governments were being greedy and attacking the natives of this world. The planet raised them up in the air, slammed them to the ground and then sent the waters that washed their bodies into the oceans. After that, both of the Animal Kingdom's leaders united and sent word to the worlds surviving leaders. Peace now. Or greater tragedy will occur. It took one hour for the world to understand what they meant. The largest sea animals I've ever seen. Kaiju. Bigger than Godzilla in the old movies, wandered up onto the shores, or out of the bottomless lakes of the enemy continents. We ambassadors met the other ambassadors that survived and informed them of the threat. If they do not stop, their entire continents would be pushed into the oceans by these creatures. They sent word to their leaderships who surrendered immediately. The Animal Kingdoms knew this was going to happen. They knew about the weightlessness. The tidal waves. They knew. And they had these massive creatures that could push continents into the ocean at any time. They had been practicing on the Isle for the entire time humans lived here, sinking it and raising it just to see how long they could keep it afloat. The whole of humanity sought treaties shortly after with the animal kingdoms. All of the nations had to rebuild their cities. The ones without governments left, fell victim to civil wars. Humanity became what they've always been. Primates.This world is much more dangerous than human-kind ever knew it to be.

I've devoted time to memories. Journaling. Drawing pictures. If anyone finds this work, and if it is helpful, I hope you see this as a way to traverse this world of Animals. Monsters. Humans and other life forms.

Welcome to Vasilias.

Log: 29880360hSE

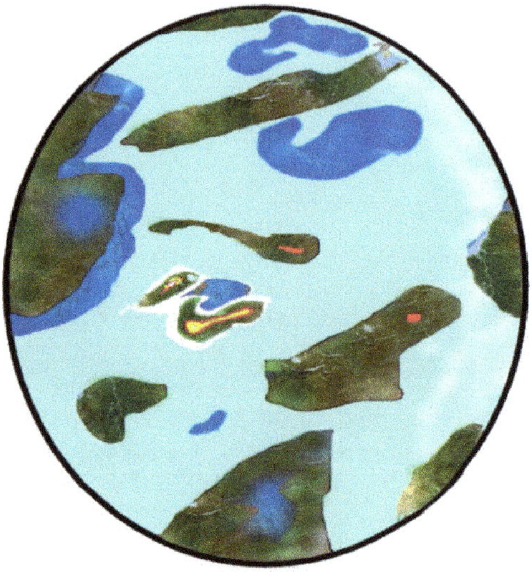

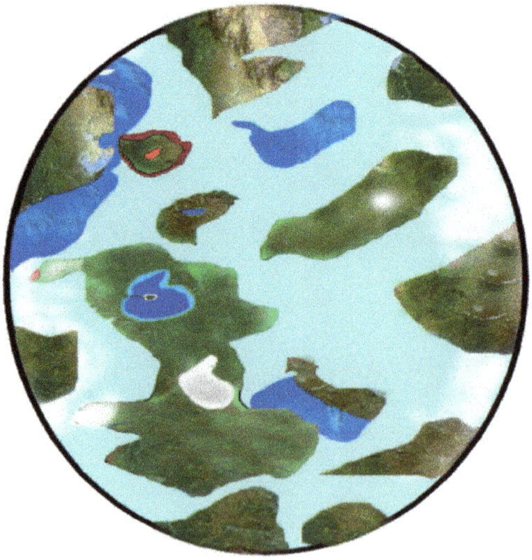

Front and back cover Model: Alexis Chalk

Photographer: Troy Conrad

Makeup artist: Latavia Thomas

Book Cover Artist: Usama Zaheen @kingof_designer on Fiverr

City Illustrator: K.L. Henriott-Jauw @Katehenriottjau on Fiverr

Newmal family Illustration: Shane Pettit

Other Illustrations: Jeremy Paul

Cartography conversion: Gis Analyst @Nadiaikram on fiverr

All rights reserved. No part of this book may be used or reproduced in any manner whatsoever without written permission except in the case of brief quotations embodied in critical articles or reviews. This book is a work of fiction. Names, characters, businesses, organizations, places, events and incidents either are the product of the author's imagination or are used fictitiously. Any resemblance to actual persons, living or dead, events, or locales is entirely coincidental.

For information contact : Jeremy Paul
PO Box 4632
Downey, Ca. 90241

http://www.kabelion.com
x.com/JeremyPaulSays

Dedicated to Uncle Steve Jordan, Aunt Lori Gartland, Cousin Marcella Rubio and friend/Memoir of an Immortal translator Ashley Zhang. Here's to hoping that whatever cure for cancer may come, comes quickly.

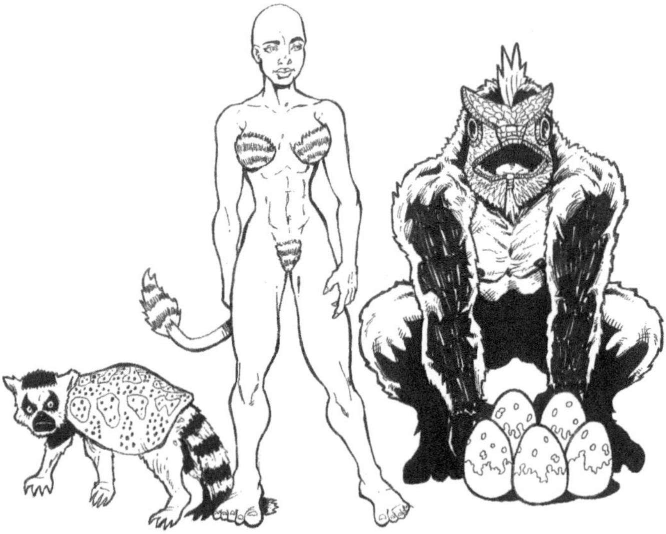

Milton Keynes UK
Ingram Content Group UK Ltd.
UKHW022014020824
446322UK00007B/24